An Earl

For Ellen

Blushing Brides
Book 1

Catherine Bilson

ISBN: 0-6481743-5-6

ISBN-13: 978-0-6481743-5-6

Other Books by Catherine Bilson

The Best Of Relations

Infamous Relations

Mr Bingley's Bride

A Christmas Miracle At Longbourn

A Marquis For Marianne

A Duke For Diana (forthcoming)

For information on forthcoming works as well as free short reads, visit my website at:

www.catherinebilson.com

Contents

Prologue 7

Chapter One 9

Chapter Two...25

Chapter Three..39

Chapter Four 55

Chapter Five 67

Chapter Six..77

Chapter Seven..87

Chapter Eight 101

Chapter Nine 111

Chapter Ten..121

Chapter Eleven..129

Chapter Twelve 143

Chapter Thirteen......................................155

Chapter Fourteen.....................................167

Chapter Fifteen..177

Chapter Sixteen 187

Chapter Seventeen 197

A Note From The Author...........................205

Prologue

December, 1817

"I'm sorry, Miss Bentley." The steward twisted his hat between his hands, an expression of genuine distress on his face. "The living's been awarded, though, and the new vicar will be arriving soon to take up residence. You've two weeks to vacate the Vicarage."

Ellen Bentley clung to the door frame, hoping it would keep her upright as her knees threatened to give way. "My father was laid to rest just this morning, Mr Ellis, and as a female I was not even permitted to stand at his graveside to offer a proper farewell. I'd hoped to seek an audience with the Earl this week." A distant cousin, the Earl of Havers did not acknowledge their relationship, but she'd planned to ask him only for a letter of recommendation for employment, perhaps assistance to find a post somewhere as a governess or companion. It was evident, however, that the Earl had no intention of allowing her to impose upon their familial connection even that much. Mr Ellis was clearly acting on his employer's orders.

I am being thrown from the only home I have ever known, was all she could think.

"I'm right sorry, Miss Bentley." The steward twisted his hat again. In her state of shock, Ellen noticed minute details; the furrow of concern between the man's beetling brows, the mist hanging in the air from his quick breathing, the way his twisting hands were damaging the hat's felt brim.

"I understand, Mr Ellis," she said quietly at last, and watched as he gave her a shallow bow before turning on his heel and retreating down the garden path.

The church bell tolled, clear in the frosty December air, and the tears Ellen had been holding back since her father's death of influenza three days earlier, not even two weeks after her mother was laid to rest in the cold ground, finally flowed.

She sank to her knees there in the doorway and bawled like a child.

What in the name of God am I going to do now?

Chapter One

Eight months later

Ellen was picking tomatoes from the vines in the garden when she heard a horse trotting along the lane, regular hoof beats punctuated by the sound of a man whistling a tune. He sounded jaunty, happy in the bright summer afternoon, and she found herself smiling, thinking that it was nice to hear someone sound so carefree.

The man came into view then, or rather his upper body did, as he rode along the lane that passed by the lodge. Spotting her over the hedge, he reined in his horse.

"Good afternoon, miss! Could you tell me if I am on the right road for Haverford Hall?"

"I'm afraid you just missed the turning, sir," Ellen said politely. "'Tis about a quarter mile back that way, on your left."

"Much obliged to you, miss!" He doffed his hat with another smile and she noticed how handsome he was, though his horse was a broken-down nag and his clothes looked worn. She smiled with a little tip of her head, but said nothing else, and he turned his horse about to ride on.

Pretty girl, Thomas thought, but he wasn't there to look at pretty girls. Riding up the long avenue lined by larch trees that led up to Haverford Hall, he paused for a moment to gaze in wonder at the building. His grandfather had described it to him many times, in loving detail, but Thomas had honestly thought the old man had been exaggerating, his memory not quite what it once was.

Now that he saw the Hall for the first time in person, Thomas realised that he had been doing his grandfather's memory a disservice, because the house was just as magnificent as he had always been told. Built of the local honey-coloured Cotswold stone, it glowed golden in the afternoon sun, windows all along the face of the building glinting in the light. He tried to count them and gave up at fifty; from his grandfather's tales he recalled the house had two large wings spreading out to the back as well, so trying to guess at the number of rooms by counting only the windows on the front elevation would grossly underestimate their number.

All this for one family, he thought, shaking his head and laughing quietly. He rattled around like a lone pea in a pod in the handsome house his grandfather had built in New York; Haverford Hall must be ten times the size, and as far as he knew it was home to only two women. And a whole passel of servants, no doubt.

Thomas sighed and pressed his weary horse to move on again; the nag nickered and flicked its ears at him. "Come on, you rotten beast," he muttered, but didn't have the heart to kick. The horse was probably nearly as old as he was, but it was the only one he'd been able to come by when the fine stallion he'd purchased in Bristol picked up a stone in his hoof and went lame ten miles from Haverford. Goliath had stumbled badly, startling Thomas who'd been riding along in a daze, and much to his embarrassment he fell off.

Scrambling to his feet covered in dust, he groaned to see Goliath standing with one hoof held high off the ground and his noble head hanging low. "Not your fault, my fine fellow," he murmured to the stallion, searching his pockets for a tool to remove the stone. Goliath was too lame to ride, so Thomas led him on to the next village, where the blacksmith was happy to take care of him but could only provide this swaybacked old mare to carry Thomas on to his destination.

He debated dismounting and leading the horse; he was arriving in a poor enough state. He'd be lucky if he wasn't turned away at the front door as an impostor. Walking his horse wasn't likely to make much difference at this stage. He had to leave her at the bottom of the imposing steps leading up to the front door, but he was quite sure she didn't have the energy to run away anyway as he mounted the steps to knock on the huge double doors.

The door was opened by a very austere-looking and formidable butler, who looked down a nose Thomas thought a great deal more aristocratic than his own and said;

"Good afternoon, my lord. We have been expecting you."

Thomas opened his mouth to identify himself and shut it again with a snap, blinking. "I... beg your pardon?"

"You *are* Lord Havers, are you not?"

"Uhhh… yes?" He couldn't quite understand how they should be expecting him today. He had left the ship immediately upon docking, and it wasn't as though they could have known he would be aboard that particular ship anyway.

The butler inclined his head regally. "Welcome home, my lord. I am Allsopp." He had his hands firmly held behind his back, and Thomas had the distinct suspicion that shaking hands with servants was not at all the done thing, so he just nodded.

"Could you have someone attend to my horse, please, Allsopp… oh," he glanced around to see the mare already being led away by a groom. "She's not mine, actually, I had to leave my horse at the smithy in Alvescot when he went lame."

"I shall let Jenkins at the stables know, my lord," Allsopp intoned, standing back away from the door in an obvious signal for Thomas to enter.

"I can see my memory will be hard pressed to recall all your names," Thomas murmured, stepping inside the house and trying not to gawk at the huge hall, panelled in dark oak, tapestries taller than a man's height hanging from the walls.

"The Countess and Lady Louisa are in the blue withdrawing-room, sir. May I conduct you there?"

Glancing down at his dusty clothes, Thomas said "I think it might be best if I just freshen up first, don't you, Allsopp?"

The man didn't crack a smile, just inclined his head slightly and said "As you wish, sir. This way, please."

"Please tell me that you're not taking me to the chambers the last Earl occupied," it occurred to Thomas to say as they proceeded up the massive staircase that led up one side of the hall.

"But of course, sir," Allsopp said placidly.

"I'd... prefer not to. Not just yet." He already felt as though he was stepping into a dead man's shoes, not that it seemed he had much choice in the matter. He'd grown up listening to Gramps' tales of the earldom, indoctrinated in the beliefs that the Earl was responsible for his people just as much as he would have been if he'd attended Eton with the sons of other aristocrats.

"As you wish, my lord," Allsopp said after a brief silence. "Several guest suites are always kept in a state of readiness, of course. Perhaps one of those will suffice?"

"Perfect," Thomas said gratefully, and Allsopp resumed ascending the stairs.

"The Cromwell Suite, I think, my lord. We will pass through the Long Gallery on the way."

He was going to need a full guided tour, Thomas could see, or he would be constantly lost. Allsopp led him into a room that seemed very nearly as large as the great hall below, and Thomas' jaw dropped.

"Now I see why you were so certain of my identity."

Portraits lined the walls, and a goodly number of the gentlemen in the paintings were very obviously related to him. Dark brown hair, a strong chin and eyes of a shade somewhere between blue and grey were apparently Havers traits that held strong through generations.

Allsopp tilted his head again. "Indeed, sir." He seemed to hesitate before gesturing to one of the paintings. "That is your grandfather Lord Matthew, I believe. The younger child, on his mother's lap."

Startled, Thomas walked closer to inspect the painting. There were three children depicted with their mother; a boy of about ten who would be Michael, Matthew's older brother, and a girl of about seven, which would make Matthew four in the painting.

"Is that Lady Eleanor?" Matthew had often talked of his sister. She had married beneath her station, to a local clergyman, but both her brothers had been too fond of her to try and deny her when she wished to follow her heart.

"The little girl? I believe so, my lord. The Countess or Lady Louisa would be able to tell you more about them."

With that it seemed he would have to be content, at least for now. Allsopp resumed his stately pace and Thomas followed along.

The Cromwell Suite was rather more luxurious than the name implied, and Thomas looked about in approval as Allsopp showed him in. "Very suitable, thank you."

"I will have someone bring hot water directly, sir. Your luggage…?"

"My trunks should arrive from Bristol tomorrow." He smiled a little guiltily. "I'm afraid I was over-eager to see Haverford Hall and to meet my family. I do have a clean shirt and breeches in my saddlebags."

"Very good, my lord," and Allsopp withdrew, leaving him alone.

Going to the window to look out, Thomas found that he was at the rear of the house, or at least on the opposite side to where he had entered. He was looking down onto a sheltered courtyard, between the two rear wings of the house, immaculately manicured gardens separated by gravel walks. A gardener was carefully pruning roses.

Everything seemed very *orderly*, Thomas found himself thinking. He'd heard stories of Americans in similar situations to himself returning to England to find their ancestral estates in ruins, having to put their entrepreneurial skills to use to rescue the family fortunes, but Haverford Hall was a far cry from ruined. What would he even do, here? Presumably the estate business was all handled by a steward, and a very efficient one from what Thomas could see.

His musings were interrupted by a knock at the door. "Come in," he called, and smiled when a young man entered and stood with his hands at his sides to offer a bow. "Hello."

"My lord. I'm Allsopp, my lord, I was your cousin Oliver's valet."

"Another Allsopp? Your father…?"

"My uncle." This Allsopp was capable of smiling, it seemed, anyway, a small grin lifting the corners of his mouth.

"It's going to confuse the dickens out of me; what's your first name?"

"Er, Kenneth, my lord, but really…"

"No buts. I shall call you Kenneth and you shall call me Thomas, because I'm already sick of being called *my lord* and I've only been on English soil since this morning."

Kenneth gaped at him. "That would be more than my job is worth, my lord!"

"Since I'm now your employer, I beg to differ." Thomas smiled at him. "Come now, it's a nice easy name. Thomas."

"… Sir?" Kenneth offered a compromise with a slightly panicked expression.

"I guess that'll do for now."

Another knock on the door announced the arrival of two burly footmen with cans of steaming water, and another came in behind them bearing his saddlebags. Idly wondering just how many servants Haverford Hall actually maintained, Thomas shrugged out of his dusty coat and allowed Kenneth to take it from him. There was a mirror hanging above the dresser on the wall; one glance in it had Thomas wincing and relieved he had made the decision to wash up before meeting the countess and her daughter. He looked even worse than he had thought after his tumble from his horse. It was a good thing that the Havers blood apparently ran strong in his veins, or Allsopp would undoubtedly have turned him away at the door like the vagrant he resembled.

Half an hour later, freshly washed, with polished boots and almost all the dust brushed from his coat, Thomas asked Kenneth to show him to the blue withdrawing-room, and received his first lesson in what jobs belonged to who in the Haverford hierarchy. Kenneth was positively shocked.

"My uncle would have my hide, sir. If you would like to go somewhere in the house, you can ask one of the footmen to conduct you until you find your way around, but to be presented to the Countess and Lady Louisa, that is my uncle's prerogative." He sent one of the footmen who had returned to collect the used wash water hurrying off with instructions to collect Allsopp at once.

"I'm going to make a lot of mistakes of this sort," Thomas said dismally as he waited. "Do you think everybody will just put it down to me being an uncouth American?"

"I'm sure they won't use the word *uncouth*, sir," Kenneth said, lips twitching very slightly, and Thomas decided that his valet did have a sense of humour, however well he might try to hide it.

"Not to my face, anyway."

"One hopes that they will not say anything so rude behind your back either, my lord," Allsopp said behind him, and Thomas almost jumped out of his skin.

"Good Lord, make a noise, man!"

"I shall endeavour to remember to do so in future, my lord."

"Does he *ever* smile?" Thomas mouthed to Kenneth as he left the room in Allsopp's imperious wake, sighing as the valet shook his head in response.

Allsopp led him back through the Long Gallery again, but turned in the opposite direction when they reached the top of the stairs, leading him into what Thomas was fairly sure was the eastern wing of the house. They proceeded past several closed doors before Allsopp came to a halt and knocked upon a door. Thomas admired the painting of a handsome bay horse hanging on the wall opposite the door, making a mental note of it as a landmark.

He didn't hear anything behind the door, but apparently Allsopp did, because he opened the door and stepped inside, intoning formally;

"The Earl of Havers."

That's me, Thomas thought with a sense of unreality coming over him. Entering the room, he stopped dead, his jaw falling open, as he came face to face with the most beautiful woman he had ever seen.

"Lady Havers, the Countess of Havers, and Lady Louisa Havers," Allsopp declared, startling Thomas and making him snap his jaw shut. He could barely drag his eyes from the vision of loveliness that had to be Lady Louisa long enough to give the countess a bow.

"It is lovely to meet you at last, my lord," the countess said formally, and Lady Louisa echoed her in a soft, musical voice.

It was an effort to keep his eyes on the older woman as Thomas said "Please, my lady, though we have never met, you are the only family I have and I am proud to claim you as such. I would be honoured if you would call me Thomas."

The countess was a handsome woman in late middle age; Thomas thought that she had once been a beauty to rival her daughter, though age had blurred the show-stopping nature of her good looks. Wearing an expensive gown in pearl-grey silk trimmed with lavender ribbons, her fair hair drawn back beneath a lace cap, she curtsied to him, the gesture somehow regal and not deferential at all.

"That is very good of you, Thomas. Perhaps you would care to call me Aunt Clarice?"

"I should be delighted." He bowed again, beginning to feel a little foolish with all the bobbing up and down, but at least he could now turn to Louisa.

"I should like you to call me Louisa," she said in that softly musical voice, smiling at him.

"I am so happy to meet you both at last," he said truthfully, staring at Louisa. She blushed prettily under his scrutiny and followed her mother's lead in seating herself; the countess gestured to a chair and Thomas sat down too, feeling gauche and awkward beside their cultured, studied grace.

He really needed to stop staring, but Louisa was beyond beautiful, she was glorious, with thick golden curls framing a pale, finely-boned face, soft red lips and deep blue eyes giving her an almost doll-like prettiness. She was no cold porcelain figurine, though, not with that lush figure that looked as though it had been poured into a lavender silk gown, a band of lace at the neckline the only thing retaining her modesty.

If dresses like that were London fashion, then Thomas was all for it. He tried to remember Louisa's age; his uncle's letters had been brief and sporadic at best, and had stopped entirely after Gramps died five years ago. Surely she was old enough to be out in society, though. He wondered why she wasn't married; but perhaps she had been just due to start a London Season when her father died. Recalled to his duty, he said;

"I must offer my most sincere condolences for the loss of the Earl and Lord Oliver. I was deeply grieved to hear of their deaths; I hope you will believe that I was perfectly content in my life in America and never for a moment coveted the earldom."

The countess inclined her head. "Thank you, Thomas. That is kind of you to say. You look very much like a Havers, I must say; Allsopp said that you saw the Long Gallery?"

"Yes, Aunt Clarice, I did, and I do hope that you or my cousin will have time to tell me who all those handsome fellows and beautiful ladies were, one day soon."

They both smiled at that. "You will have to have your own likeness taken," Louisa said.

"I suppose so." It hadn't occurred to him.

"Sir Thomas Lawrence is a very fine painter; he recently competed a portrait of Louisa which hangs now in the music room," the countess offered. "Perhaps you could commission him to take your likeness."

"Perhaps, but after painting Louisa, surely all the rest of us mere mortals must look as ugly as mules to his eyes," Thomas said.

Louisa blushed again and looked down at her lap. Busy staring at her, Thomas didn't notice the countess's satisfied smile.

Chapter Two

"I believe I have some news that may be of interest to you, my dear," Mr Bledsloe announced at dinner, two evenings after Ellen had seen the stranger riding along the lane.

"Well, do not keep us in suspense!" Demelza cried, setting down her fork. "Tell us all, Mr Bledsloe, and quickly, if you please!" She smiled at Ellen, inviting her to rejoice in the juicy gossip which was no doubt about to be imparted. Ellen smiled weakly in reply, not wishing to offend, but Mama had abhorred gossip. As a parson's wife, she came by a goodly amount of secrets, but she had always said that words had the power to be harmful.

"Sticks and stones may indeed break your bones, but words most certainly do have the power to hurt as well," Mama had told Ellen. "People trust me with their secrets, and I will not betray that trust."

Mr Bledsloe paused importantly, and then declared "The Earl of Havers has arrived at Haverford Hall."

Ellen relaxed; that was surely not a secret that could hurt anyone. The whole village had been on tenterhooks for months, wondering when or even if the American cousin would come to claim his title. As eager as Demelza for information, she hushed her friend, who was squealing with excitement and fanning herself.

"When did he arrive, Mr Bledsloe? Have you seen him?"

"Apparently, he came to the Hall the day before yesterday. The butcher's apprentice is walking out with one of the downstairs maids at the Hall and he saw her on her half-day yesterday; she said that the Hall's servants are all abuzz about it."

"Oh," Ellen said, surprised, "I think I saw him, perhaps, riding along the lane. He asked directions to Haverford Hall."

"Then you *spoke* to him, not *saw* him, you silly clunch! Was he handsome?" Demelza leaned forward eagerly.

Ellen blushed, thinking that she had indeed been struck by the good looks of the man who had asked her for directions. "I am sure I could not say," she said demurely. "I only saw him briefly, riding his horse. He spoke to me over the garden hedge. I do not even know if it was the Earl; it might have been a servant, perhaps, who came with him. He was riding an old hack of a horse, and his coat did not look as expensive as those that the old Earl or Lord Oliver used to wear."

"I shall go up to the Hall and seek an audience with him tomorrow," Mr Bledsloe said importantly. "I have some papers the old Earl entrusted to me. I shall mention you to him then, Ellen."

She said nothing, just quietly carried on eating her dinner. She was nothing to the new Earl; a distant, penniless cousin. He was obliged to do nothing at all for her, and considering the attitude of every member of the aristocracy she had ever met, was likely to consider her no more importance than the dirt on his shoe... that is, of absolutely no importance and to be scraped off at the earliest opportunity.

Once Mr Bledsloe had confirmed that the Earl had no interest in her, she would begin tomorrow to look more seriously for paid work. She would ask Mr Bledsloe for his newspapers and begin writing letters applying for situations as a governess or companion. It was time to earn her keep.

Eating his breakfast and managing to miss his mouth with his fork more often than not because he couldn't stop gazing at Lady Louisa, demurely nibbling on a buttered scone, Thomas was startled when the butler announced that he had a visitor.

"Who is it?" Thomas asked, discarding his napkin and rising, almost relieved for an excuse to stop making a fool of himself. He'd already smeared jam over his chin twice.

"The local solicitor, Mr Bledsloe," Allsopp intoned formally.

"He can have no business with you, Thomas dear," the countess said. "My husband conducted all his legal matters through our London solicitors, of course. Send him away, Allsopp."

"No, I'll see him, Aunt Clarice. He is a neighbour, after all."

Lady Havers blinked at him, apparently quite bemused. "I do not know how things are done in America, Thomas, but here neighbours are other members of the gentry, not *solicitors*."

The scorn in her voice made Thomas blink. Gently, he said "In America, neighbours are the folks who live close by and who we see regularly, ma'am. No matter what their station in life." Turning away, he said "Lead the way, Allsopp. To... uh..." He hadn't the faintest idea where one received visitors of any rank at all.

"The study, my lord." Allsopp actually cracked a little smile. "This way, if you please."

"I actually think I can find the study," Thomas said cheerfully to Allsopp as they left the small dining room where he'd leaned the family customarily ate breakfast. "It's down that corridor and just past the really short suit of armour, right?"

"Correct, my lord." Allsopp didn't smile again, but Thomas was sure the butler was beginning to unbend. He'd get a chuckle from the man yet.

"And Mr Bledsloe, what can you tell me about him?"

"He is very well-respected in the local area, my lord." Allsopp paused before saying "Far be it from me to contradict the Countess, but Mr Bledsloe and the Earl met often. The Earl was also the local magistrate, you see. And the Bledsloe house is just past the end of the southern avenue approaching the Hall."

29

"Then he *is* a neighbour," Thomas said triumphantly. "Very good, Allsopp. Would it be appropriate to have coffee sent in?"

"Certainly, my lord. I shall have it brought in shortly."

"Thank you." Thomas smiled as Allsopp looked faintly startled; the servants were definitely not used to being thanked, but Thomas had no intention of changing his habits of courtesy now that he happened to have a title tacked onto his name. Opening the study door, he entered the room with a ready smile.

"Mr Bledsloe! I am delighted to meet you, sir."

The solicitor was a stout man in early middle age, his hair thinning. He jumped to his feet as Thomas entered, his expression quite shocked at Thomas' friendly greeting. Bowing, he stuttered "Uh, very good of you, my lord, very good indeed. I'm honoured that you'd see me."

"Nonsense, we're neighbours, and please call me Havers," Thomas said affably. He was trying for a charm offensive; if he could catch the man by surprise at the beginning of their acquaintance, perhaps he could convince him that all the bowing and scraping really wasn't necessary.

"Uh, yes, my l-Havers," Bledsloe said, his eyes wide and a little shocked. "Honoured." He accepted Thomas's offered hand and shook.

"Good, that's settled. Do sit down." Instead of rounding the huge desk and sitting imposingly behind it, Thomas caught up another chair and sat down near Bledsloe. "It's very good of you to call. I'm delighted to start meeting my new neighbours."

"Neighbours? Why, yes... I suppose we are."

"Allsopp tells me that you live at the end of the southern avenue, which must surely make you one of our closest neighbours, since the northern approach is three times as long, I'm told."

"Not quite at the end, my l-Havers. A little further along the road towards Colesbourne. In fact, I believe you may have spoken to a young lady in my garden the day you arrived, asking directions?"

"The girl in the grey bonnet! A relative of yours?" Thomas nodded, remembering the girl and her smile, the friendly way she had spoken to him.

"A friend of my wife, actually; she is staying with us for a while, since the loss of her parents. They both passed in the same tragic manner as your uncle and cousin. For which losses, please allow me to extend my condolences."

31

"Thank you," Thomas said with a nod. "That must have been difficult, for a young girl to lose her parents both at the same time. I suffered the same loss, but I was not old enough to remember their passing; my grandfather raised me."

"That would be Lord Matthew?"

"That's right. He raised me on tales of Haverford," Thomas smiled, looking around. "I'm afraid the images my imagination produced did not do it justice, though."

"Indeed." Mr Bledsloe paused, and then said "Did Lord Matthew ever speak of his sister?"

"Lady Eleanor? Frequently! I think he missed her most of all when he emigrated. They wrote letters until her death, I believe, but that was before I was born. In fact, perhaps you can tell me—I know she married, but did she have children? I have not yet had the chance to ask my aunt about other living relatives I may have, indeed I am just getting used to having *any*!"

"Quite understandable, my lord. And yes, Lady Eleanor did have a daughter. In fact, if I may?" Bledsloe gestured to a bookshelf behind the desk, and Thomas nodded, watching curiously as the man stood and pulled down a large, old-looking book richly bound in gold-embossed leather.

"This is the Havers family bible. The fourth Earl, that was the previous Earl's father, of course, and your grandfather's older brother, kept it updated until his death not quite twenty years ago."

Thomas nodded in understanding as Bledsloe laid the book on the desk and carefully opened it to the back pages, showing a family tree written out in several different hands.

"Ah, this will be useful when I am trying to keep straight who is who in the portraits in the Long Gallery," Thomas murmured thoughtfully, leaning forward to look.

"Here, you see," Bledsloe pointed. "The fourth Earl and his siblings, Matthew and Eleanor."

A line led down from Matthew to *Ellis (b. 1767, m. 1789, d.1792)*. Written beneath his name was *Julia Henry, (d.1792)* and another line led down from there to *Thomas (b. 1790)*.

"You can, of course, write *6th Earl Havers* in beside your name now," Bledsloe said.

"Perhaps another day." Everything in Thomas rebelled against that, right now. Maybe he'd leave it to a descendant who didn't feel like a complete impostor. He looked across the family tree and realised that he would also have to write in the dates of death for Michael and Oliver.

No, he wasn't not ready to deal with that right now either. He moved his finger back to Eleanor's name, and down from there.

"She had two daughters… oh, one died young, how sad." Five years old, Miss Sarah Ripley had been. Looking at the dates, he realised that must have been the same year Gramps had left for America. Had little Sarah died before or after his departure? What a terrible year that must have been for Eleanor.

"Yes, but Miss Laura survived to adulthood. She married a Bristol merchant, and they had a daughter, Susan. On a visit to her relatives here in Haverford, Miss Susan fell in love with the local curate and they married. Following the wedding, the fourth Earl bestowed the living on Mr Bentley, so that his relative Susan should be sure of a comfortable life."

Thomas listened with interest as Bledsloe told him about the family he had never known. Following the line written in a spidery hand in the back of the old bible, he came to *Ellen (b. 1798)*. The same year as Louisa on the other branch of the family tree, he noted.

"Did the fifth Earl keep the family tree updated?" he asked.

"He wrote in your grandfather's date of death, so I assume so. So far as I know, there were no other records that required noting during his stewardship of the title."

"So Ellen is still alive?"

"Ellen is the young lady I told you about, Havers. Susan Bentley was her mother."

Thomas fairly gaped at him, eyes flying back to the family tree. In all the myriad branches, so far as he could see, there were only three Havers descendants living; himself, Louisa, and Ellen. "Why is she staying with your wife, then, and not here with her family?" he demanded indignantly.

Bledsloe hesitated, and then said delicately "While the fourth earl considered Lady Eleanor's descendants to be family and bestowed the living on Mr Bentley to ensure that Miss Susan should be taken care of, the fifth earl did not."

Thomas sat back and looked at the other man. "You're saying that the previous earl—hang it, I'm just going to call him my uncle—did not acknowledge Susan and Ellen Bentley as relations?"

"May I speak frankly?"

"Please do, because I have the feeling that I'm missing something here. From what I see here, we hardly *have* any family." Thomas waved his hand over the book. "Why would my uncle not acknowledge the perfectly respectable wife of a clergyman and her daughter?"

"Because your uncle was a penny-pinching man who never did a thing unless he thought it benefited him." Bledsloe looked half-defiant, half-afraid as he said the words.

A knock on the door interrupted them, a maid bringing in a tray with a steaming pot of coffee. Thomas poured a cup for Bledsloe and one for himself, grateful for the interruption since it gave him time to gather his thoughts.

"What provision was made for Ellen when her parents died?" Thomas asked.

"She inherited savings of some one hundred and seventy pounds," Bledsloe said. "Though her grandfather was quite a successful merchant in Bristol, he married again after his first wife died and had two sons, who inherited his wealth. The living was awarded to another man; signing those papers was one of your uncle's last acts, as it happens." Bledsloe looked down, bit his lip. "Ellen intends to seek a position as a governess, or companion. We asked her to stay on with us at least until your arrival; she has been helping my wife with the children. While we cannot afford to pay her a proper wage, she eats with the family and Demelza treats her like a sister."

Like an unpaid governess, you mean, Thomas thought a little unkindly, but he suspected that Bledsloe's guilt over the matter was the reason why the solicitor had approached him now.

"It seems entirely unfair that my cousin should be forced to make a living for herself in this way," he said aloud. "She is twenty, by the date here?"

"Indeed."

"Should she like to marry? If there is a suitor in the wings for her, I would happily provide a dowry?"

"The only suitor who has ever asked for her is the new parson," Bledsloe said. "He seemed to think that she should be grateful for an opportunity to stay in her old home, though it meant she would also have to be his unpaid housekeeper and warm his bed. Since he is some five and fifty years old, however, I advised Ellen against it. She did seriously consider it, though. She does not wish to be a burden upon anyone."

"I am already thinking that I do not like the new parson," Thomas said after a moment of stunned silence. "What is his name?"

"Mr Brownlee. He has already found another wife, a daughter of one of your tenant farmers who was quite happy to accept his offer."

Shaking his head, Thomas considered his options. The easiest thing to do would be to settle some money on Ellen, but then what? Where would she live? She would need to find a companion of her own, to lend her countenance. Would she even want that, or accept the money?

"I believe that I should like to meet Ellen," he said finally, after taking a long sip of his coffee. "We spoke only briefly when she gave me directions to the Hall, but she seemed quite charming. She is my cousin no less than Lady Louisa, and I should like to know her."

"Very good, Havers." Bled sloe gave him an approving nod. "When would be convenient for you?"

"No time like the present, Gramps always used to say. May I walk back with you?"

Chapter Three

It was a very pleasant walk along the avenue between the larch trees. Thomas found himself whistling again, enjoying the weather.

"Is it always this pleasant here in September?" he asked.

"Not always, this is a very fine late summer," Bledsloe said. "October rains will start soon enough, and the nights start drawing in. How is the climate in New York, Havers? I have heard that the winters can be very bitter."

"Indeed, with heavy snowfall at times," Thomas agreed. "Summers are unbearably hot, too; I was not sorry to leave in May, before the weather became too hot. I understand the English climate to be milder all around."

They talked about the weather, about the harvests, and about the work Bledsloe had done with the previous earl as they walked. Bledsloe said that another local landowner, Sir Thomas Kingsley, had been appointed magistrate after the earl's demise, for which Thomas was grateful; he would have quite enough on his plate without needing to worry about enforcing the law in the area as well!

At last they came to the end of the half-mile-long avenue and Bledsloe turned towards the house Thomas had passed the other day. He remembered thinking it looked quite a nice property, on an acre or so of grounds with a large kitchen garden to one side, where he had spied Ellen picking fruit. Bledsloe pushed open the wooden gate and they walked up to the front door.

"Demelza will likely carry on a little bit," Bledsloe said in an undertone. "Don't mind her nonsense. She likes to fuss, that's all."

Seeing the smile on the man's face, Thomas thought that he seemed very fond of his wife despite any fussing. At least Ellen was in a home where she need not fear importuning by the master of the house, a very real fear if she should indeed go into service as a governess or companion.

"Demelza? I have brought a visitor to meet you, my dear," Bledsloe said, leading Thomas into a parlour where a pretty woman of about thirty years sat with two children, both listening intently as their mother read to them. "Boys, stand up and give your best bows, now. This is the Earl of Havers. My lord, my wife and my two sons, Jacob and Jason."

The boys were twins, he saw, of about seven years or so, quite identical in their blue-eyed, fair-haired, freckled little faces, quite open-mouthed with awe at the sight of a real live earl there in their parlour.

Demelza Bledsloe gave a little shriek and dropped her book. "John! Oh, my lord!" she curtsied a little frantically. "I never… oh my goodness!"

"Please, do not be put out, Mrs Bledsloe," Thomas turned on the charm offensive again, stepping forward to lift her hand and kiss it. "I do beg your pardon for my dropping in on you unannounced, but when your husband was good enough to pay a call upon me I decided that I simply could not wait to return it—and to meet my relative, who I understand is your very dear friend."

"Yes, where is Ellen, my dear?"

"Oh, she is in the morning-room," Demelza fluttered a little, settled down as Thomas gave her a calm smile. "She found a notice in yesterday's newspaper with a position she thought might suit, said that she wished to write an application letter—I did tell her to wait until after John had spoken with you, my lord, but she was so certain you would not be interested in even meeting such a distant relative…"

"On the contrary, ma'am, I am most interested in meeting Miss Bentley. So far as I know, I only have two living blood relatives, Miss Bentley and Lady Louisa. I am not of a mind to snub one of them for any reason." He tried to look reassuring.

"That is very good to hear; I knew it must be so! I heard that Americans have quite a different way of thinking than we English, well, to the aristocracy at least. Please, my lord, do not let me keep you; the boys have not yet finished their geography lesson. Perhaps we shall all come and have tea together in the morning-room shortly?"

Thomas allowed that sounded very pleasant, smiled at the twins whose faces had turned immediately downcast at the mention of the temporarily abandoned lesson. Emboldened by his smile, one of them—he had no idea which—blurted "Have you ever seen a Red Indian, m'lord?"

"Perhaps if your mother tells me that you have paid close attention for the remainder of your lesson,

I will tell you when we take tea," Thomas bent down to whisper, was rewarded with a pair of beaming smiles.

Cute little devils, he thought, taking a polite leave of Mrs Bledsloe and following her husband from the room. He'd not thought seriously yet about taking a wife and setting up a nursery—he was only twenty-eight!—but he supposed that he must now view it as his duty to do so, and as soon as possible. The earldom needed an heir.

The next door along the small hallway stood open, into a room of similar size to the parlour, an oval table to seat eight or so in the centre of it. Ellen sat at the table, papers spread out before her and a quill pen held in her hand.

"Ellen?" Bledsloe said. She looked up, her eyes widening at the sight of Thomas entering the room behind him.

"Oh!" Startled, she set down her pen, rose to her feet and made a graceful curtsy.

"The Earl of Havers, pray allow me to present Miss Ellen Bentley," Bledsloe said formally, and then with a smile, "your cousin."

"It is quite a distant connection, my lord," Ellen rushed to say.

"I know exactly how distant, Miss Bentley; your great-grandmother was my grandfather's dear sister. He told me many stories of Lady Eleanor, and I am delighted to meet her descendant." Thomas bowed, giving Ellen a reassuring smile. She looked troubled, her brow furrowed.

"I'll just step to the kitchen and ask Betsy to see about that tea," Bledsloe said, "let you two get acquainted." Leaving the room, he left the door standing wide open and Ellen and Thomas staring at each other in silence.

She was prettier than he'd thought with that ugly grey bonnet obscuring her hair, Thomas realised, though the plain dark grey gown she wore did nothing for her. She was still in mourning for her parents, of course, but then so was Lady Louisa for her father, and she had managed to find a gown that flattered her.

As soon as he thought it, Thomas kicked himself for such insensitivity. Louisa had an unlimited budget and probably a seamstress dedicated to her wardrobe, whereas Ellen had only a paltry legacy. Undoubtedly she was making do with whatever she had.

"Won't you sit down, my lord?" Ellen said eventually, taking a seat herself. Thomas sat down, still taking her in. She looked thin, although Bledsloe had said she ate with the family. There were hollows in her pale cheeks and shadows beneath her eyes, a dark chocolate colour quite unlike his own blue-grey. Her hair was darker than his, almost black, though the sunlight pouring in through the window behind her brought out some mahogany-red glints in it. He saw little resemblance in her features to either his own or Louisa, and wondered if she resembled her Havers grandmother at all, or whether her looks favoured a different part of her family.

"Bledsloe told me something of your situation," Thomas said awkwardly after a moment of silence. Ellen was just sitting, her hands folded in her lap, not looking at him. "I am very sorry to hear of the loss of your parents."

"I am sorry for your loss too, my lord."

He blinked in confusion.

"The Earl and Lord Oliver?" she prompted.

"Oh, I see. I never knew them, I'm afraid. My grandfather corresponded with them to some extent while he was still alive, but since his death five years ago I heard not a word until a representative from my uncle's London solicitor contacted me in New York."

"I see," Ellen said colourlessly, and there was another brief silence before she said "Do you have other family, back in America?"

"No, my parents died when I was very young. A fire. Gramps raised me."

She nodded silently, and Thomas wondered where the friendly, smiling girl he had seen in the garden just two days ago had gone. *She didn't know who I was then,* he realised in a flash of enlightenment. *She's afraid of me, of how my actions may upset her little world.*

"May I call you Ellen?" Thomas asked, trying to make his voice as quiet and gentle as he could. "And I should like it if you will call me Thomas, if you will. I have only three living relatives in this whole world, and you are one of them."

Wide eyes lifted to his face, and he noticed lighter amber glints in the dark chocolate of her eyes. She said nothing for a long moment before finally saying "I do not want to appear disrespectful in front of others, but I suppose if we are in private conversation, as we are now, I could call you Thomas."

"There, that wasn't so hard, was it?"

She smiled at last in response to his teasing tone. "Not so hard. I have never had a cousin before."

That raised his eyebrows. "Of course you do. Lady Louisa…"

"I have seen Lady Louisa every Sunday at church since we were both old enough to attend and I am quite sure she has no idea what my name is."

Thomas sat back, studied her thoughtfully.

Ellen looked down at her hands, biting her lip guiltily. "I should probably not have said that," she murmured. It had been decidedly snippy and un-Christian. Her mother would have sent her to wash her mouth out with soap.

"No, you have every right to be resentful. I can hardly believe the way the family has treated you myself. That changes now."

Her eyes were still wary as she looked at him. "What do you mean?"

"What do you want, Ellen?"

"Excuse me?" Startled, she blinked at him.

"What do *you* want? To do with your life, I mean? What are your dreams, what could you do if you could do anything at all?"

She hesitated, staring at him. "I… don't know. Nobody ever asked me that question before. I don't think it's a question that many girls are asked, really. We are expected to want nothing more than to be a wife and mother to some man…"

47

"That's not what you want?"

"Maybe." A tinge of colour touched her pale cheeks. "I haven't ever met a man who made me want those things."

"Fair enough." Thomas steepled his fingers, tapped his fingertips together thoughtfully. "Do I take it, then, that becoming a governess or a schoolteacher, or companion to some wealthy lady, is not in fact your life's ultimate dream?"

"It is not. Until this meeting, though, I thought it was the only future that might possibly be open to me!"

"Are you happy here?" he asked, seeing that she seemed a little more relaxed and easy with him.

"Here?" She looked puzzled. "In Haverford? I have never known anywhere else."

"Staying with your friends, I mean. Mr and Mrs Bledsloe."

"Oh, I see... well, Demelza has been so very kind. I had nowhere else to go after Mr Ellis told me I had two weeks to vacate the Vicarage."

Arrested, Thomas blinked. "Wait. What, Mr Ellis, the steward?"

"That's right."

"My uncle's steward... ordered you out of your home? Within days of your parents' deaths?"

"The very day of Papa's funeral. Mama died two weeks before... she was not very strong, and once she died I think Papa just gave up the will to live." Ellen blinked back tears, remembering those awful weeks. She had fallen ill first, and was just recovering when Mama caught the illness. Exhausted and still recovering herself, Ellen did her best to nurse her mother, but to no avail.

"I'm so sorry," Thomas said. "I can't believe Ellis took that upon himself."

"Oh, Thomas." She gave him a world-weary look. "Mr Ellis would never have taken any such action without the direction of the Earl. I had already moved here by the time I heard that the Earl himself had caught the influenza and fallen ill."

Thomas buried his head in his hands, feeling utterly ashamed of his late relative. "Dear Lord, how could he be so cruel? To you, to a young female relative, all alone in the world?"

Ellen had no answer for him. She had asked herself that question many times, how a man who called himself Christian, who attended church, could behave in such a way.

"I think you should come and live at the Hall." Thomas dropped his hands from his face to look at her again. She gaped at him in utmost astonishment.

"I… do not think that the Countess would care for that very much."

"Since it is not her house, I do not particularly care what she thinks," Thomas said sharply. "Do not tell me that *she* could not have done anything for you, even if her husband was the veriest miser! I saw the household accounts yesterday; a single month's worth of her pin money could have purchased you a cottage of your own outright!"

He seemed quite outraged on her behalf. There was really nothing Ellen could say; she just sat looking at him, hands folded in her lap.

"I am below the age of majority," she finally offered hesitantly. "I suppose… technically, as my closest relative, you are my legal guardian."

"Am I?"

"We could ask John. He is a solicitor, after all, I am sure he could advise on the legality of the matter." Ellen gave him a little smile. "Thomas, truly, I am grateful that you want to do something for me. I don't really want to be a governess or a companion. I suppose I had always hoped I would find some nice gentleman farmer or perhaps a curate who liked me well enough to offer for me."

"If that's what you wish, Ellen, I will see that you are introduced to every gentleman farmer and curate in England until you find the one who can make you happy," he promised.

She actually giggled at such a ridiculous statement, hand flying up to cover her mouth, her eyes sparkling. "I am sure it would not take so very many!"

Delighted to have made her laugh, Thomas smiled broadly at her. "Is it settled, then? You will come to live at the Hall… with your family?"

She nibbled on her lower lip, considering it. "I think that you should speak with the countess first," she said carefully at last. "While you are of course correct that it is your house, I do not wish to be the cause of contention between you and your family."

"If I do, will you prepare to remove to the Hall within the next few days?"

She nodded at last. "I will. And Thomas… thank you."

Reaching across the table, he took her hand between both of his and pressed it gently. "We are *family*, Ellen. That means something to me, and I should have wished to see you comfortable even if I had not inherited the title. My grandfather made himself quite the fortune in the Americas, you know."

"Did he?" Ellen looked genuinely interested. "I should very much like to hear about your grandfather."

"He was a character, to be sure. I'd be delighted to tell you some of his stories. He was your relative too, after all."

Footsteps at the door made Thomas let go of her hands and look around; the twins came darting in, their mother behind her and John Bledsloe on their heels with a tray in his hands.

Any serious conversation had to be cut short as the boys promptly annexed Thomas and bombarded him with questions about America. Laughing, he attempted to answer them as best he could while Demelza poured tea and handed around a plate of biscuits.

Walking back up to the Hall an hour later, it occurred to Thomas that he had not enjoyed himself so much in a very long time. Ellen had relaxed further with her friends in the room, and he had enjoyed hearing her merry giggle ring out at the twins' antics. The two boys were obviously very fond of her, and she of them. After a little while, Bledsloe had quietly asked Thomas to step out, and the two men adjourned to a small study to converse privately.

Thomas began to whistle again as he walked. Bledsloe had indicated his pleasure that Thomas wished to bring Ellen into the bosom of the Havers family.

"We shall be sorry to lose her, I know Demelza quite relies upon her, but it is not fair to Ellen. She is a good, sweet girl and she deserves the opportunity to make something of her life. I must say, Havers, I am very glad that you are not of the same mind as your late relative in this matter."

Thomas was honestly ashamed that a relation of his could have treated a blameless young woman so shabbily. Ellen clearly had no great expectations, but his uncle could have made her life comfortable with barely any inconvenience to himself. Why, a dowry of a few hundred pounds would have had every gentleman farmer and curate in the county queueing up to court Ellen!

Merely dowering her did not feel like enough to Thomas now that he had met Ellen, though. Doing so would push her down that narrow path into marriage, and he wondered if she even wanted that. As she had said, women were rarely asked what they wanted from life, it was merely *expected* of them that they would want to be wives and mothers.

Ellen deserved a chance to discover what she really wanted to be in life, and by God, Thomas was going to give it to her.

Chapter Four

"You want to *what*?" Clarice's voice rose shrilly as she stared at Thomas, her eyes wide with incredulity.

"I want our cousin to come and live here at Havers Hall." He kept his voice even, glancing sideways at Louisa as he spoke. She was sitting with a piece of embroidery in her hands, but had not placed a stitch since he began speaking. Her face was as still and cool as a marble statue; he could not read what she was thinking.

"She is a vicar's daughter."

"She is *my cousin.*"

They stared at each other in a silent battle of wills, Clarice every inch the noblewoman. Thomas finally broke the deadlock by saying;

"I am not asking your permission, Aunt Clarice. Should you find that you are unable to reside beneath the same roof as Miss Bentley, you have life rights to the Dower House as stipulated in your marriage settlements, I believe."

Clarice's mouth opened with shock. Louisa made a small sound, and when Thomas looked back at her, he found that she had laid down her embroidery and was looking at him directly.

"Of course that will not be necessary, Thomas," she said in her sweet voice, smiling at him. "I am delighted by the opportunity to get to know Miss Bentley. As you say, she is my cousin too. We shall be pleased to welcome her to the Hall, will we not, Mama?"

Relieved that Louisa was on his side, and pleased by her compassion and eagerness to meet Ellen, Thomas smiled happily at her. She returned her attention to her embroidery, a smile playing about her lips, becoming colour in her cheeks.

My God, she is so beautiful.

Lost in gazing at Louisa, Thomas barely noticed Clarice's put-upon sigh, and her eventual remark of "Fine, then. If you *must*."

Clarice's reaction once Thomas had left the room was telling, however. She rose from her chair and stalked up and down, scowling. "I cannot believe he means to foist off this girl upon us!"

"He is American, Mama," Louisa placidly set another stitch. "I understand they have very different ideas about the lower classes, indeed they do not seem to think that there *are* any lower classes."

"Utter nonsense," Clarice harrumphed. "There is a natural order to things. Bringing Miss Bentley to live here indeed! Whatever will he do next? The sooner he comes to his senses and marries you, the better."

"These things cannot be rushed, Mama," Louisa snipped a trailing end of thread neatly. "You told me that. Slowly, softly, so that he does not know he is in the trap until it is already closed. He is already sniffing about, ready to take the bait."

"Must you speak in those crass hunting terms, Louisa? You sound positively bloodthirsty." Clarice wrinkled her nose with distaste. "Be very sure that you do not allow Thomas to know you have a ruthless side until you have his ring upon your finger, my dear."

"Never fear, Mama. I have things well in hand. Miss Bentley will be no obstacle to our plans, I assure you."

Mollified and reassured by her daughter's calmness, Clarice sighed and took a seat again. "Very well, dear. For your sake I shall try to pretend I am pleased by the girl's presence."

"I do not think that you need to go that far, Mama. Let me befriend her while you act as though you tolerate her merely because Thomas has ordered it. She will want a friend and she will soon be willing to do anything I ask, never fear."

"And then what?"

"Why, then I find some suitor to marry her and take her off our hands." Louisa shrugged. "Thomas can dower her with a few hundred pounds or so, and we will have minor squires crawling all over her in eagerness to be connected to the Havers family."

"Hm." Clarice looked thoughtful at that. "I suppose she might even be useful, that way. I shall have a think about who might be suitable."

"As you say, Mama." Louisa picked up her handiwork and resumed stitching, the very image of a well-bred lady filling her time.

For the second time in the space of a year Ellen found herself uprooted, but this time she was moving up in the world. She had never been closer to Haverford Hall than seeing it in the distance when walking up Wyck Beacon; the Earl had not exactly been the type to welcome the residents of the village to his home. It truly was quite magnificent, she thought as she walked up the avenue, Demelza beside her holding her hand, John slightly ahead of them.

Thomas had sent a baggage cart to collect her belongings and invited the Bledsloes to accompany her to tea, doubtless hoping that their presence might help ease her transition to residing at the Hall. He had stopped by almost every day during the previous week, assuring her that the countess and Lady Louisa were eager to welcome her to the Hall, asking when she could be ready to move. His enthusiasm was irresistible, and Ellen found herself quite excited about what the future might now hold for her.

As they approached the Hall, however, Ellen found herself holding tighter to Demelza's hand.

"Just remember, you belong here," Demelza said in an undertone as they walked up to the great doors. "You were named for Lady Eleanor, your great-grandmother, who was born under this very roof. You have every right to be here."

59

Sucking in a deep breath, Ellen squeezed one more time before letting go of her friend's hand. She would not be seen clinging on like a child to her nursemaid.

The door opened almost immediately upon John's knock to reveal a formally-garbed, stern-faced butler. Ellen knew who he was, of course; the Allsopp family had been in Haverford as long as the noble family they served, and she had seen Allsopp in church on many occasions.

"Good afternoon, Mr Bledsloe, Mrs Bledsloe," Allsopp intoned, and then to Ellen's surprise, he bowed to her. "A very great pleasure to have you here at last, Miss Bentley."

Was Allsopp *smiling*? Stunned, Ellen mumbled something unintelligible in response. She hadn't even thought the poker-faced butler knew *how* to smile.

"The family are gathered in the Oriental sitting-room," Allsopp informed them. "Please, allow me to escort you there."

Another shock; Ellen would have thought that task might be delegated to a footman, but apparently they—*she*—was considered a significant enough guest to merit Allsopp's personal attention.

Thomas fairly leaped to his feet as the party entered the sitting-room, beaming a smile. "Here you are!"

"Havers." Bledsloe shook his hand in greeting, bowed formally to the countess and Lady Louisa, who were rising to their feet. "Lady Havers, Lady Louisa."

"Mr Bledsloe." Clarice nodded regally at him. "I do not recall that your wife has ever been presented to me."

Demelza was not in the least overawed. "We have seen each other many times in church, your ladyship," she said rather dryly, dipping into a curtsy that was just barely low enough to show respect to a peeress.

Clarice's smile looked as though it had been painted on, but she said nothing else as John presented Demelza to her and Louisa. Louisa at least seemed more friendly, saying;

"A pleasure to make your acquaintance, Mrs Bledsloe."

"As it is yours, Lady Louisa."

Ellen hung back, biting on her lip, but Thomas would have none of it. Seizing her hand, he placed it on his arm and led her forward.

"I know you will wish to join me in welcoming Ellen to our home, Aunt."

"Of course." Clarice inclined her head graciously. "Though, Thomas dear, you really must remember to call her Miss Bentley when we are in company. Really, are all Americans so informal?"

"Most of them are considerably less formal than I, Aunt Clarice," Thomas replied with a chuckle. "Consider the advantages, though; any error in address I may make will not reflect badly upon you. Indeed, you can commiserate with the offended party while informing them that I am merely an ignorant American!"

There was a distinct bite to his words; Clarice, far from accepting the rebuke, merely sniffed. "You *are* an Earl. The number of those who could rightfully be offended by any informality in your address are few in number. I was merely thinking of Miss Bentley's reputation. Over-familiarity in address must be avoided for her sake, lest assumptions be made."

Louisa tittered behind her hand, and Thomas, who had been about to ask what kind of *assumptions* Clarice could mean, closed his mouth. A young lady's reputation was all-important, and in England the rules of etiquette were even stricter than in America, he had already worked that out.

"Yes, Aunt Clarice," he said penitently at last.

Ellen had not said a word since entering the room. She took advantage of the silence that fell now to curtsy and say;

"I am honoured to make your acquaintance, Your Ladyship."

Clarice inclined her head regally, before tilting her head to the side and considering Ellen thoughtfully. "You have the Havers colouring. And the Havers nose."

Ellen's hand rose instinctively to touch the feature remarked upon, before she lowered it again. "So I have been told."

"I have only seen a portrait of your great-grandmother Lady Eleanor as a child," Thomas put in, "but perhaps there is a picture of her in later life, somewhere in the collection?"

"You are quite correct, cousin," Louisa said, smiling sweetly at Ellen. "It is in the music room on the ground floor. Cousin Ellen, I must say that you resemble her quite strongly."

Ellen smiled back, relieved that the other girl seemed disposed to be friendly. "I should be pleased to see it, if you would care to show me, Lady Louisa."

"Not right now, dear, we are going to have tea. Sit here by me, if you please," Clarice said, her tone making it clear that she was giving an order. Thomas frowned at his aunt, but Ellen made no objection, merely taking the indicated seat with a smile on her face and every indication of being honoured at Clarice showing her attention.

"How are you enjoying Gloucestershire, my lord?" Demelza enquired then. "You are aware, perhaps, that the Cotswolds are considered one of the greatest beauties of England? Is there anything to compare to them in America?"

Thomas smiled, turning to her. "The area is indeed very beautiful, and quite different to what I am used to. America is vast and very diverse in landscape, though I regret to say I have travelled very little. I did go once with my grandfather to see the great waterfall at Niagara, which was quite the most spectacular sight I have ever seen."

"I saw a drawing of the falls once," Ellen said surprisingly. "Is it not where Bonaparte's brother honeymooned with his first wife?"

Everyone in the room stared at her. Ellen's cheeks coloured. "Sometimes Papa used to show me the newspapers and discuss things with me," she mumbled.

"Ladies of quality do not read the newspapers, dear," Clarice said patronisingly. Thomas saw Ellen's eyes flash with rebellion for an instant before she lowered them to her hands, clasped in her lap. He immediately made a silent promise to himself to see to it that Ellen had the opportunity to peruse the newspapers whenever she wished, and to discuss them with him, too. She probably had a far greater understanding of current affairs in England then he did.

"Is it true that mountains of ice float in the ocean?" Demelza changed the subject gracefully.

"I have heard so, but did not see them on my voyage to England. Of course, I was lucky enough to be making the crossing at the height of summer; winter crossings are much more perilous, I understand," Thomas turned to her with a smile.

Chapter Five

After the tea, at which Thomas and Demelza carried the conversation with little input from the others, John and Demelza took their leave and Clarice summoned a maid to show Ellen to her room while Thomas escorted John and Demelza out.

"Susan will be your personal maid, Miss Bentley," Clarice said, gesturing to the girl sunk in so low a curtsy her knees almost touched the floor. "She has been well trained as a lady's maid. I trust you will find her to your satisfaction."

"I had not expected such generosity as to have a maid assigned to me at all, my lady," Ellen said. "Indeed, it is entirely unnecessary. I am quite accustomed to making shift for myself."

Louisa tittered a little behind her hand; Clarice merely elevated her head a little higher. "That would be quite unsuitable," was all she said, and the conversation was at an end.

Haverford Hall was a maze, Ellen discovered as she followed Susan along apparently interminable corridors. She knew that the Hall had been built in several stages, the earliest part dating back to the fourteenth century and subsequent owners adding onto it until it reached its present size.

"I believe I may need a map, Susan," she said in an attempt at humour as they finally reached her new room. Or *rooms*, as she soon discovered when Susan opened the door to show her inside; she had a private sitting-room, a dressing-room and a bedroom beyond that.

"You'll soon find your way about, Miss Bentley," Susan said shyly. "Besides, I've a bed in your dressing-room; I can take you anywhere you want to go until you have your bearings."

Grateful for the consideration, Ellen nodded. Susan had already unpacked her belongings, she could see; hung her few gowns in one of the closets. They looked meagre and pathetic in the large space, and that was only one of the closets.

A knock on the door to the sitting-room made Ellen turn; she was half-way over to open it herself when Susan rushed past her, wide-eyed with panic.

"Oh no, Miss Bentley, you must let me get that!"

Apparently, she was not supposed to do anything for herself. Ellen found herself wondering just what exactly she *was* supposed to do as Susan opened the door to reveal Thomas standing outside.

"Do you like the rooms?" Thomas asked as soon as Susan admitted him. "I think Aunt Clarice would have put you up in the attics with the kitchen-maids if she could, but Louisa suggested this guest suite. They call it the Yellow Room."

Ellen could see why; the furniture was all upholstered in a soft shade of golden yellow, which matched the fittings on the bed. Fortunately, whoever had selected the decorations had an eye for subtlety and had not gone too overboard with the colour.

"They are very pretty rooms, I thank you," she said honestly. "Far grander than what I was expecting. I do not doubt that even the servants' rooms in the attics are quite comfortable."

"Not so much as I would like," Thomas said unexpectedly. "I inspected them this morning. I will not have my staff living in meagre conditions while I wallow in luxury; I will be ordering several new beds and chairs, and I intend to instruct the housekeeper to ensure that extra blankets are available for anybody who asks for them. I have been cold, New York is bitter in the wintertime, and I would not have anyone suffer that if I can prevent it."

Susan gave Thomas a look that was near-worshipful. "That is very good of you, my lord," she said timidly. "I shared one of those rooms with my sister Agnes until her ladyship said I was to move in here and do for Miss Bentley. I was right worried about her being cold this winter."

"Nobody at Haverford Hall will go cold this winter, and that is a promise," Thomas said firmly. "Nor in Haverford village, if I have my way. Ellen, it strikes me that as the vicar's daughter you very likely know all the residents and their needs far better than my aunt does."

"I doubt Lady Havers knows anyone with any *needs*," Ellen said unguardedly, before clapping a hand over her mouth. "I beg your pardon. I should not have said that," she mumbled through her fingers, her cheeks bright red.

"Why not? It's almost certainly true. Aunt Clarice does her very best to only associate with the upper echelons of society; I have known her barely a week and that much is quite obvious. Neither she nor Lady Louisa have ever visited the tenants, charitably or otherwise, I understand from the housekeeper, and I have to say that I do not approve. It does not fit with the stories Gramps used to tell me about the responsibilities of the earldom; he told me he regularly used to escort his mother and his sister about on their visits."

"I should like to hear about that," Ellen said eagerly. She glanced at Susan, who took her cue.

"Could I ring for some refreshments for you, Miss Bentley, m'lord?"

"We just had tea, thank you... what is your name?"

"Susan, m'lord," she gave him a deeply respectful curtsy.

"Perhaps you might just sit over there by the door, which we shall leave open? To give Lord Havers and myself countenance if anyone should happen by," Ellen suggested, saw Thomas' puzzled frown. "We cannot speak in private in a room with a closed door," she advised him gently. "Even though we are cousins and I am technically your ward."

"I see."

She wasn't sure that he did. Considering what she suspected of Lady Louisa's motives towards him, she wasn't too sure that his aunt and his other cousin could be relied upon to ensure he understood *all* the rules of polite society, either.

"You would escape censure, but my reputation could be irretrievably damaged," Ellen warned. "You should never allow yourself to be alone with any unmarried female, Thomas, lest you find yourself confronted by an angry father bound and determined on making you marry her. I don't have one of those," her smile was sad, "so I would just be ruined. As relations we have a little more leeway than most, but you should bear in mind that there are plenty of ladies who would seek to entrap you into marriage. You are wealthy, titled, young and handsome. Avoid being alone anywhere."

"Lest a young lady suddenly join me, and we be found together mere moments later by an enraged father?" Thomas understood what Ellen was getting at. Shaking his head at the idea of such manipulation, he smiled suddenly. "You and I shall have to shield each other; you can protect me from marriage-minded misses and I can protect you from the young men who will no doubt swarm about you!"

Ellen blinked. "What young men?"

"When we go to London, of course."

"London?" She stared at him in incredulity. "What do you mean, when *we* go to London?"

Thomas opened and closed his mouth several times, finally taking on a rather sheepish expression. "In all the kerfuffle of getting you moved here, I have just realized that I have neglected to apprise you of the plans my aunt has been making," he said. "The Little Season is under way at the present time, and she thinks that now would be a good time for me to get my feet wet in the deep waters of London society. The household will remove to the Havers townhouse in Belgravia in ten days' time."

Ellen was silent for a little while, considering. It was clear that her options were limited; she supposed that if she made enough fuss, she might be permitted to stay with John and Demelza while the others went to London, but if she were being honest, she had always dreamed of seeing the capital.

"We are still in mourning," she said at last.

"True, but it has been more than half a year. Aunt Clarice and Louisa have set aside their blacks and greys for violet and lavender; you could do the same." He gave her an encouraging smile. "You would look charming in lavender."

She laughed, thinking of the contents of her wardrobe. Every dress she had was one that she had made over, either from one of her mother's or one of her own. Most of them were black, dyed from their original colours when she entered mourning. The others were carefully saved awaiting the day when she would put it off. There was nothing lavender or violet among them. Nor could she borrow anything from Louisa or Lady Havers, even if they would lend it to her; she was taller by a handsbreath than either of them, and any of their gowns on her would show far too much ankle.

"What is funny?" Thomas gave her a quizzical look.

"I have nothing suitable to be seen in London, cousin. My gowns mark me as the poor relation here; there, it will be assumed I am a servant attached to your household." She gave him a direct look. "You know very well I am penniless, so what is your plan?"

"You and I will both need new wardrobes," Thomas replied, apparently unconcerned. "Fashions are slightly different in London than New York, I believe, and I do not wish to appear the unlettered colonial. Aunt Clarice and Louisa are already making plans to order new gowns for themselves; all bills will be sent to me. I have no doubt that Aunt Clarice will be happy to advise you as to what you should order."

Ellen did not feel nearly so certain of that, but once again, she supposed that she had little choice. Consider it an adventure, she told herself. How many times did you daydream of going to London, of seeing places you have only read about in books and newspapers?

"I must say that I am looking forward to seeing London very much," Thomas said, unconsciously echoing her thoughts. "I have read so much about it!"

Ellen smiled at him. "So am I, Thomas. Tell me, what do you wish to see first?"

Chapter Six

Ellen could hardly believe the amount of baggage Lady Clarice seemed to think was necessary to remove the household to London for a few weeks. Trunk after trunk was packed and loaded onto a procession of baggage carts, despite both Clarice and Louisa continually discussing the entire new wardrobes they planned to order for themselves once they reached the city.

Thomas actually came out and said what Ellen was thinking, when he cast an appalled eye over the mountain of trunks already strapped to one of the carts.

"What are you planning to do with all these things, Aunt? You have enough clothes packed here to wear three different outfits every day in London;

shall I take it then that you do not plan to visit the modistes after all?"

Clarice looked down her long nose at him and sniffed. "You know nothing about London fashions, Thomas, nor of what is required to ensure that our family remains in the first circles of society."

"True," Thomas admitted with a sigh. "Very well, Aunt Clarice. Do as you see fit."

"I shall." Turning her head away from him, she called "Careful with that bandbox, man! My favourite hat is in it!"

"Yes, your ladyship," the hapless footman she was addressing replied.

"Come," Ellen touched Thomas's arm. "Will you walk with me, Cousin?"

"Indeed, I believe a walk would be just the thing right now." Thomas shook his head. "All this... I packed my clothes and moved *continents* on a few days' notice, with no expectation of ever returning to my old home. Everything I absolutely, positively could not live without fit into just two trunks."

Ellen said nothing as they walked along one of the curving paths that led through the Hall's famous rose garden. All her belongings, treasured or otherwise, hadn't filled the single trunk she had borrowed from Demelza to transport them to the

Hall. She could not ever imagine owning as many beautiful gowns as Louisa and Clarice possessed, never mind desiring any more.

"Are you looking forward to London?" Thomas asked. "To having some new gowns and meeting new people?"

"I do not particularly care for new gowns," Ellen said, "though Lady Havers insists that I must have them, and I will accept her advice on the matter. I would not for the world bring shame upon the family, even though I am in truth a poor relation."

"You are *not* a poor relation," Thomas said firmly. "You are one of the only living members of the Havers family."

"The poorest one."

"For now." He smiled mysteriously and would say no more, even when Ellen pressed him. They had become quite friendly in the few days she had resided at the Hall. It transpired that they both liked to rise early in the morning, and regularly encountered each other in the breakfast room. Thomas had surprised her on the very first day by asking if she would like to see the library; Ellen agreed eagerly and was delighted when he oh-so-casually pointed out a table in the large room and remarked that the newspapers were always left there once he had done perusing them.

"Allsopp has instructions not to dispose of them for seven days," Thomas said, "just in case I should think of something I would wish to review, of course."

"Of course," Ellen echoed in wonder, looking around the library. She had never imagined that so many books could even exist, never mind be kept all in one room. There had to be thousands of volumes on the oaken shelves.

Following her gaze, Thomas said "It appears that the previous Earl was an inveterate reader. Much of the collection was added during his lifetime, I understand. You are welcome to borrow any book which takes your fancy, Ellen."

He had no idea of the magnitude of the gift he had just given her, Ellen knew. She could not adequately express her gratitude, but she tried, stumbling over her words until Thomas took her hand in his and pressed his fingers on it lightly.

"Havers Hall is your home now, Ellen. This is your library as much as mine. You have no need to thank me."

She knew he was wrong about that, but he would not hear her exclamations, only shaking his head and saying that he would leave her to look about at her leisure.

Every morning since then, they had breakfasted together and Thomas took the time to ask her what she was reading, and discuss it with her. He was well-read, Ellen had discovered; apparently he had attended the American university of Harvard, which Americans considered just as good as Oxford or Cambridge. Nor was he dismissive of her opinions just because of her gender, which was a first for her. Even her father had occasionally told her that she could not possibly understand something simply because she was female.

Ellen hoped that they would be able to continue their morning routine in London. "Does the London house have a library?" she thought to ask as she and Thomas turned about on their walk to return to the Hall.

"I should be very surprised if it does not, though perhaps it may not be quite as extensive as the one here at the Hall. Consider, though, the opportunities London offers for shopping! I have no doubt that there will be plenty of bookshops; if we find the library at the townhouse inadequate, we shall have plenty of opportunity to improve it."

Ellen smiled at his enthusiasm. "You shall be too busy, surely, joining gentleman's clubs and giving speeches in the House of Lords."

"How shall I contribute sensibly in the House of Lords if I do not read the news and talk it over with you, Ellen?" Thomas laughed at her. "I am not too sure that English gentlemen will be interested in socialising with an uncouth American, besides."

He was nervous, Ellen realised with incredulity. "Of course they will," she said robustly, "all of the neighbouring gentry who have come to meet you have been very friendly."

Havers Hall had been positively swarmed with everyone who could think of a good excuse to call, all eager to meet and curry favour with the new Earl. Thomas had insisted on presenting Ellen to everyone as well, even though many of them already knew her and looked askance at Thomas presenting her as his cousin, equally with Lady Louisa. None of them wanted to offend Thomas, though, so they were all polite, at least publicly, though she had seen a few sneers directed her way when Thomas' attention was elsewhere.

"The baggage carts are ready to depart, my lord, with your approval," Allsopp met them on their re-entry into the Hall.

"Of course, if everything my aunt wants has been packed," Thomas nodded. The carts were being sent ahead so that everything would be already in

London when they arrived; the family would not depart until the following morning and planned to spend two days travelling. Lady Clarice had already arranged for them to spend their nights with noble families who resided along their route; no roadside inns for the Havers family.

Ellen was not particularly looking forward to spending two days in a carriage in company with Lady Clarice and Lady Louisa. Thomas had already announced his intention to ride his stallion for most of the journey, at least so long as the weather remained clement. Peering up at the sky as they entered the Hall, Ellen sent up a silent prayer for rain. Thomas' presence in the carriage would make the journey a great deal more bearable. Clarice and Louisa did not criticise her directly, but she always felt as though she was being judged and found wanting when their cool blue eyes fell upon her.

On the other hand, sitting in the carriage watching Thomas and Louisa making calf eyes at each other didn't appeal all that much, either.

She walked down to the village that afternoon to visit John and Demelza, to farewell them before her trip. A footman and her maid escorted her and waited to walk her back; despite Ellen's laughing protests that she had been walking alone all over

Haverford since she was let off leading strings, on this matter Thomas had sided with Lady Clarice, who threw up her hands in horror at the thought. So Ellen just did her best to pretend that the two servants weren't there, walking ahead and humming softly under her breath, enjoying the crispness of the air on the pleasant September day.

"Ellen!" Demelza exclaimed over her with all her customary warmth, but her sharp eyes could see that something was bothering her younger friend. Deflecting her children with promises of cake in half an hour if they would play quietly until then, she drew Ellen into the parlour and closed the door. "Darling, what's the matter?

Ellen tried to protest that everything was fine, but she crumbled under the pressure of Demelza's genuine, gentle concern, and ended up confessing all her fears and worries about going to London.

"… and I just *know* that everyone will look at me and see me for the poor country cousin I am," Ellen ran down finally, and Demelza rose and took her in a warm, comforting embrace.

"They will see you for the charming, caring, beautiful young woman that you are," she reassured. "You will be a hit in London, Ellen; I don't doubt that you will come back engaged to a duke or someone terribly important who has recognised you as a treasure beyond compare."

Ellen laughed through the lump in her throat. "I don't think I'd make a very good duchess."

"You would be magnificent," Demelza said loyally. "You *will* be magnificent. Promise that you will write and tell me all about it?"

"I shall write so often you will spend all your allowance on paying for the postage and write back begging me to stop." Ellen had to hold back tears as Demelza hugged her close.

"Never," Demelza promised. "John would never grudge me your letters, dearest. You shall write as much as you wish, and I will write back, though our dull lives will be of little interest."

"Oh, never say so," Ellen smiled through her teary eyes. "Your recounting of the boys' antics will keep me greatly entertained, I am sure!"

A crash in the next room made them both wince. "Talking of which," Demelza said with a sigh, "I knew it was too good to be true."

"Come, they are eager for their cake, and you have reassured me." Ellen smiled bravely, and her friend took her hand, squeezed it.

"You will be fine, dearest. Just be yourself, and you will soon make friends."

Ellen could only hope Demelza was correct.

Chapter Seven

Demelza's words came back to Ellen as she looked around the crowded ballroom, and she smiled ruefully. Her friend had never even been to London, had no idea of the ways of high society. Beauty, wealth and connections were the only coin the *Ton* recognised, and Ellen had none of the first two and little of the last. She had visited the fashionable modiste Lady Clarice patronised, allowed herself to be draped in silks and satins, measured and pinned for gowns more luxuriant than anything she had ever imagined. The first night wearing one of her new gowns, she had truly felt like a princess as she entered the ballroom just a step behind Louisa.

By the end of the night, the scales had well and truly fallen from her eyes. Thomas was the only man who had asked Ellen to dance while Louisa was constantly surrounded by a crowd of gentlemen three deep clamouring for her attention. None of them had given Ellen more than a second glance. This was the third ball she had attended as part of the Havers family, and she had still only ever danced duty dances with Thomas.

Sipping on a cup of punch she had been forced to ask a footman to procure for her, it occurred to Ellen that she was, in fact, a confirmed wallflower. Relegated to the fringes of the room where matrons sat on uncomfortable chairs and gossiped about the gathered throng, she might as well have been invisible.

With a quiet sigh, Ellen found a seat for herself. Her new dancing slippers pinched her toes and she was glad to sit down and ease her feet.

"Hello," a friendly voice said, and she looked to her left, her eyes widening as she took in the beauty of the woman sitting beside her. Around the same age as Ellen herself, she guessed, the lady wore a gown in the first stare of fashion, a choker of impossibly large diamonds around her slender throat, a mass of red-gold curls artfully arranged atop her head.

"Er, hello," Ellen stuttered, a little awe-struck by the lady's beauty. Why in the world was someone who looked like that sitting alone at the side of the room engaging complete strangers in conversation? She should be on the dance floor, being fawned over by a horde of swains even larger than Louisa's.

A handsome young gentleman paused in front of them, making the lady an impeccable bow. "Might I implore you for a dance, Lady Creighton?"

The lady's smile vanished instantly. "Thank you, I do not care to dance," she said, not meeting his eyes.

"May I fetch you something? A glass of punch?"

"I thank you, no." Deliberately, Lady Creighton lifted her fan, snapped it open and turned her head to the side, looking at Ellen and hiding her face from the gentleman. He bowed, his expression melancholy, before backing away.

"Did you know him?" Ellen asked impulsively.

"Only slightly," Lady Creighton said with a sigh, lowering her fan and checking that the gentleman had truly left them alone. Her foot was tapping along to the music, Ellen saw.

"But you did not wish to dance with him?" Curiosity roused, Ellen quite realised that she was being rude, but she couldn't help herself.

"I am not permitted to dance with anyone except my husband," Lady Creighton said with another sigh, "nor to converse with any gentleman when I am not in his presence."

Ellen's eyes widened with shock. "I... see," she said at last, thinking that the lady's husband must be very jealous.

"So I find events like this dreadfully tedious, since generally after the first dance my husband abandons me to my own devices and heads for the card room."

The lady was lonely, Ellen realised. She offered her a friendly smile. "He does not object to your conversing with other ladies, though?"

"Fortunately, no. I am Marianne, by the way."

"Ellen Bentley... Lady Creighton?"

"Countess of Creighton, for my sins." Marianne's smile was weary. "It is a pleasure to make your acquaintance, Miss Bentley. You do not dance tonight?"

"I did dance," Ellen said a little defensively. "The second dance, with my cousin, the Earl of Havers."

90

"How nice."

"…And since then, nobody has asked me," Ellen confessed. "I'm a wallflower, I'm afraid."

"Which is quite ridiculous, for you're very pretty, and cousin to an Earl."

"The poor relation, I'm afraid," Ellen smiled, but she couldn't quite hide her hurt. Thomas had promised, after all, that she would be treated equally to the rest of the Havers family. She could hardly blame him for the way other people treated her, though, and how was he to know? He was from America, and no more familiar with London society and its unspoken rules than she.

Marianne tilted her head curiously. "What difference does that make?"

"I'm sorry, but I don't understand what you mean."

"Allow me to share a story with you," Marianne said. "Once upon a time, there was a gentleman with an unfortunate habit of losing at the card tables. Without particular connections of his own, he had entrée into the higher circles of society through his wife's family."

Spellbound and wondering who the gentleman in the story was, Ellen listened in silence.

"One day, the gentleman sat down to a game of cards at his club which was particularly ill-fated. By the end of it, he had lost every possession he ever owned and his opponents held notes of debt he could never hope to meet. He was a pauper. Desperate, he approached the only connection he had who might offer him aid in his time of need; his late wife's distant cousin, the Earl of Creighton." Marianne's lovely face was emotionless as she continued. "The gentleman had only one thing left to offer the Earl; his eighteen-year-old daughter, accounted a very pretty girl by all who saw her. Indeed, her first London season was turning out a smashing success. Miss Abingdon was courted by quite a number of eligible gentlemen, all of whom were willing to overlook her lack of dowry and her father's well-known habits. Their suits all came to naught, however, when Mr Abingdon accepted the Earl of Creighton's offer for her."

Marianne's expression was remote as she finished her little story. Ellen did not quite know what to say. Miss Abingdon was evidently Marianne herself.

"So, you see," Marianne said after a few moments of silence, "wealth and connections are not required in order to catch a husband, even one among the wealthiest and most highly titled in the land.

There are plenty of gentlemen out there with their own fortunes, in charge of their own destinies, and I cannot at all comprehend why some of them are not looking at you and seeing a lovely young woman who would make some lucky gentleman a fine wife."

Put like that, Ellen supposed it was a little odd that nobody at all approached her. There were plenty of plainer girls than she, of no greater wealth and in many cases lesser family, who regularly appeared on the dance floor on the arms of eligible young men.

"Even Miss Brightling dances more than you, and she is afflicted with eyes that cross, protruding teeth and an insatiable appetite for sweets which has given her a girth similar to that of a horse," Marianne said, accurately if a little cruelly. "Why does Lady Havers not introduce you to some of the young men buzzing about her daughter? There would not be enough dances for Lady Louisa to give them one each if this ball lasted until tomorrow night."

"I suppose... maybe Lady Havers does not want me distracting from Louisa's limelight?" Ellen said uncertainly. Although she was uncertain why Louisa apparently needed suitors at all; her play for Thomas had been both obvious and apparently successful. Thomas stood glowering jealously at Louisa's group even now. Poor Thomas; every time

Louisa smiled at one of her swains he looked most distressed. Ellen wished that she might say or do something to comfort him.

"The Earl needs to stop pining after Lady Louisa and start making acquaintances of his own social circle," Marianne said. "I'm afraid that I may not speak to him to effect introductions, but there are some ladies I might introduce *you* to, if you would be willing? They have relatives near to your cousin's age who are upstanding young men."

The slightly wistful tone in Marianne's voice made Ellen wonder if the young men in question had been among her suitors before she was married off to Creighton. Grateful for her condescension, though, Ellen said honestly that she should be delighted to make any new acquaintances.

"Excellent. Do come with me." Rising gracefully to her feet, Marianne led Ellen along the wall to where a group of older society matrons were gathered. "Lady Jersey, Lady Sale, Mrs Peabody. May I introduce Miss Ellen Bentley to your notice? She is a cousin of the new Earl of Havers."

"An American?" Lady Sale said sharply. She had a long, narrow nose, and a way of looking down it that made Ellen feel very small.

"No, my lady, I was born and raised in Haverford," Ellen dipped a curtsy. "I am quite a distant cousin," she said with devastating honesty, "my great-grandmother was sister to the Earl's grandfather."

"Quite close enough," Lady Jersey said with a hearty chuckle. "My great-grandmother was mistress to one of our former monarchs, and my family has never quite managed to live down the scandal!"

"Sally!" Lady Sale shook her head, but a smile curved her thin lips upward as Mrs Peabody let out a high, girlish giggle.

A little shocked, Ellen blushed, saw that Marianne was blushing too. Lady Jersey was examining her now with a critical eye.

"You're here with Clarice, I suppose?"

"Lady Havers, yes, my lady," Ellen nodded.

"Never did like her. Why isn't she introducing you about, hm? Worried you'll be competition for her daughter, Laura is it?"

"Lady Louisa," Mrs Peabody corrected her.

Lady Jersey waved a plump, beringed hand carelessly in the other woman's direction. "Yes, yes, Lady Louisa, we all know the type. Diamond of the first water and all that. Why didn't she find a husband in her first two seasons, hm?"

"Holding out for a bigger fish," Lady Sale said knowledgeably.

The other ladies hummed in acknowledgement before all looking back at Ellen.

"You did well to bring her to us, Lady Creighton," Lady Jersey nodded to Marianne.

"I hoped. My situation means that I cannot be of much use, but you ladies... well, you were very kind to me at my debut."

"You quite broke poor Tristan's heart when you married Creighton, my dear," Lady Sale said, "but I never blamed you. *We* know what kind of man your father was."

Looking past them, Marianne paled suddenly. "Excuse me," she said hastily, and walked briskly away to join a gentleman who had just entered the ballroom.

"Poor girl," Lady Sale and Mrs Peabody said almost in unison while Lady Jersey was not nearly so restrained.

"Wasted!" she snapped.

"Is that Lord Creighton?" Ellen asked shyly, a little horrified. The earl, if it were he, had to be at least seventy years old if not more, almost entirely bald, his face deeply wrinkled. He was a big man, though, tall and still powerfully built despite his age, and as

Marianne hastened to his side he put out a large hand and clamped it tightly around her wrist, almost dragging her from the room.

"Unfortunately, yes," Lady Jersey said, "and if Clarice has her way, you'll probably end up married off to someone just as awful. Let us see to thwarting her plans, my dears. Regrettably, Almack's is closed until the Season proper or I should provide you with vouchers, but Town is not entirely devoid of suitable prospects at this time of year." She gave Ellen a warm smile, raking her from head to foot with sharp eyes. "At least Clarice has seen fit to outfit you properly, although lavender isn't quite your colour. Why are you still in mourning, if the previous earl was such a distant cousin?"

"My parents both passed away last December," Ellen said, once again having to swallow the painful lump in her throat. She did not think that she would ever stop missing them.

"Oh, you poor dear!" Mrs Peabody said sympathetically. "I must introduce you to my godson. Now where is that boy…"

"Edmund is far too young to be looking for a wife, Agatha," Lady Jersey said firmly. "Nice boy, but still at Oxford," she informed Ellen. "You need a man already set up; I take it you don't have your heart set on a title or one of England's great fortunes?"

"Just a simple home of my own and a man with a kind heart," Ellen said. "I grew up in the parsonage at Haverford, my lady; my expectations are humble."

"Humble, indeed!" Lady Sale gave her an approving look and the other two nodded. "Well, perhaps we can do a little better than that. Would you have any objections to a military man? The Wares' second son is in the Navy and has lately received promotion to a captaincy and his own ship…" without waiting for Ellen's reply, she waved to a sturdy young man in uniform and soon recruited him to dance the next set with her.

While Captain Ware was pleasant enough, he did not seem particularly interested in making more than polite conversation. Ellen was nevertheless pleased to dance at all, and grateful to the ladies for their condescension. Upon the conclusion of the set, Captain Ware returned her to her new benefactresses, where Ellen was surprised to find that they already had another partner awaiting her. Lord Bellmere was duly introduced, politely enquired as to whether she was engaged for the dance, and upon hearing that she was not, escorted her to the line of couples.

Beginning to enjoy herself despite the new dancing slippers still pinching her toes, Ellen smiled at Lord Bellmere when he asked how she was enjoying London.

"Oh, a good deal, my lord! Though I have not as yet had an opportunity to go to the British Museum; I am hoping that my cousin will be able to arrange a visit for us soon. I am very eager to see the famous marbles which Lord Elgin brought back from Athens."

Lord Bellmere, a softly-spoken gentleman in his early forties who had not particularly objected when his cousin Lady Sale caught his attention and insisted he danced with a country nobody, found himself intrigued. In his experience, the Elgin Marbles and the British Museum were not generally the attractions which young ladies found of particular interest on their first visit to London.

"I have a friend who is on the board of the Museum," he offered. "While the public opening times are a sad crush, it is possible to obtain tickets to more exclusive viewings. I could see if my friend might be able to assist…?"

Ellen's smile was quite radiant as the dance brought them back together to clasp hands and bow.

"Why, Lord Bellmere, that is a most generous offer! Thank you so much!"

Miss Bentley was very pretty when she smiled like that, Lord Bellmere thought, deciding that he would pay a call on his friend on the morrow. And that he owed his cousin Lady Sale a thank-you, for bringing Miss Bentley to his attention. No dowry to speak of, Lady Sale had said, but he was comfortably off and had no need of a wealthy wife. A pretty one with a brain between her ears, someone who would not bore him to tears in conversation, would suit him very well.

"Might I call upon you, Miss Bentley?" he enquired.

A pretty colour flushed Ellen's cheeks as the dance ended and they bowed to each other. "That would be very pleasant, Lord Bellmere."

Chapter Eight

Partnering the pretty wife of another young Earl he had lately been introduced to in the dancing, Thomas was surprised to see Ellen join the set with a gentleman he did not know. Ellen looked happy, smiling and talking animatedly with her partner, and the gentleman seemed equally taken with her.

"Pardon me, Lady Hallam," Thomas said, "but do you see the couple three down from us in the set, the beautiful dark-haired lady in the lavender dress with the green sash…"

"I see them, but I do not know her, if you are angling for an introduction," Lady Hallam said with a cheerful laugh.

"That is my cousin Miss Bentley, ma'am. I was just wondering if you knew her partner?"

"Ah! Indeed, I do, that is Lord Bellmere. One of the Duke of Northumberland's grandsons; there are a whole collection of them, and though he's a long way from the ducal coronet he has a baronetcy from his mother and a very nice estate near Warwick, I believe." She cast another look at the pair as the dance took them around to face Ellen and her partner. "Your cousin seems to have caught his fancy. He's a very respectable gentleman, I assure you. No scandals or black sheep in that family."

The news should have pleased Thomas, but he found himself frowning as he saw Ellen smiling widely at her partner again. What was the man saying, to make her look so pleased? He had not thought Ellen the type to fall for empty flattery. At the end of the dance, he hastily returned an amused Lady Hallam to her husband and set off in search of Ellen, finding her just as the next dance started.

"El-Miss Bentley," he said.

"Cousin," she offered him a pretty curtsy and a smile. "I pray you will excuse me; Major Trevithick has just engaged me for this dance."

The very tall, very thin redheaded gentleman on whose arm Ellen's gloved hand daintily rested, gave him a polite bow. There was little Thomas could do but smile and nod, though he found himself frowning after Ellen as she and her partner joined the forming set.

"So you're Havers," a voice said behind him, and he turned to find himself the focus of several pairs of beady eyes.

"At your service," he bowed, unsure of the protocol. They had not been formally introduced, but then one of the ladies had addressed him, and from their jewels and gowns these were the kind of highly-ranked ladies who could sneer at convention all they pleased. Bellmere was standing with them, he noticed, and the baronet stepped forward.

"I'm Bellmere, my lord; I just had the pleasure of a dance with your charming cousin Miss Bentley."

"Yes," Thomas said, deciding quite irrationally that he did not like the shape of the other man's eyebrows. Recognising that he was being slightly ridiculous, he forced himself to smile and be polite as Bellmere introduced Lady Jersey, Lady Sale and Mrs Peabody. Having read the newspapers diligently since his arrival in England, and not merely the political pages but the society ones as well, he recognised the names as some of the leaders of the *Ton*. Apparently, they had taken a liking to Ellen, because no sooner had they been introduced than they started telling him—not asking, but telling—that they intended to take her on and see her well married.

"Ellen—ah, Miss Bentley—is my ward, yes," he answered a question from Lady Sale, "but she is in the charge of my aunt the Countess."

"Clarice has her hands full with Lady Louisa and her army of suitors," Lady Jersey said with a sniff, "whereas here we are, three bored dowagers with not a single girl between us to bring out this season. Lady Havers hasn't had a minute to introduce Miss Bentley to anyone, Havers—do you mind if I call you Havers?"

"Would it matter if I did?"

"Not in the least, dear boy." She smiled at him. "You may be American, but clearly you're not a fool."

There wasn't much he could say to that, so he just bowed politely. Clearly Lady Jersey was a law unto herself.

"Thank you for your attentions to my cousin, milady. I will assume that you have her best interests at heart."

"Don't worry about a thing, Havers," Lady Jersey waved a hand weighed down with gem-studded rings. "We'll have her married off in no time."

Thomas found that he could not feel as enthused about that idea as Lady Jersey and her friends seemed to be. "I will have to approve any serious suitors for her hand, of course," he said stiffly, "and I trust that you will not introduce her to any gentlemen who are unsuitable."

Lady Jersey gave him a penetrating look, but it was Mrs Peabody who asked;

"And do you have any particular criteria for suitability, my lord?"

Lord Bellmere hadn't made himself scarce, Thomas noted, and was listening avidly to the conversation.

"No gamblers, or heavy drinkers," Thomas said, trying to think of a good reason to exclude Bellmere apart from his detestable eyebrows. His age, that had to count against him. "A gentleman with his own property, but not too high in the instep; Miss Bentley's father was a parson and she was raised quite simply."

"Pshaw," Lady Sale said sharply, "my father was a parson too, and I managed perfectly well when I married Sale."

"The *Marquess* of Sale," Mrs Peabody murmured, for Thomas' edification.

"Your pardon, my lady, I meant no offence." He offered the marchioness a deep bow, and she sniffed, looking slightly mollified.

From the corner of his eye, Thomas caught a glimpse of Ellen and her tall partner in the dance. The man's red coat, clashing with his hair, gave him another idea.

"While I have the utmost respect for the courage of England's brave soldiers, I am not sure that I should care to see Miss Bentley married to a military man, either. The necessities of military service must needs keep them apart, and happiness in a marriage is difficult to achieve in such cases." He carefully didn't look at Lord Bellmere as he added one final recommendation. "Finally, I should prefer Ellen to marry a man reasonably close to her own age."

"Well, we shall take all those things into account, Havers," Lady Jersey said, sharp eyes boring into him. "For the most part, they are not unreasonable things to want for your cousin. I note that you did not mention her preference, though. Are we to take that into account and deny her if she discovers a partiality, for example, for naval captains?"

Thomas had the uneasy feeling that she was teasing him, though he could not discern precisely

106

how. "Miss Bentley's happiness is my first concern," he said.

"Of course."

Lady Jersey was definitely laughing in her sleeve about him, and Lady Sale and Mrs Peabody looked quite unaccountably amused as well. Bellmere was eyeing him in a peculiar way, almost as though sizing him up.

Deciding that retreat, in this case, would be well-advised, Thomas politely excused himself and made his way back across the room, glimpsing Ellen and her partner again on the way. Ellen was smiling again, that happy, bright smile he had only ever glimpsed a few times, usually in the library at Haverford when she discussed a particularly interesting book with him.

Was Ellen truly enjoying the ball so much? Thomas could not say that he was; so far, the people he had met had been dull, sycophantic or both, for the most part. The three older ladies he had just met were by far the most interesting encounters of the night.

"I say, Havers," a hand caught at his sleeve and he paused, recognising Viscount Danbury, a gentleman around his own age who he had met earlier in the week. Two other young men were with Danbury, smiling at him in welcome.

"Danbury," Thomas acknowledged. He had the distinct suspicion that the other man's only interest in him was because of his relationship to Lady Louisa; Danbury had been very quick to trade on their brief acquaintance to claim an introduction and a place on Louisa's dance card.

"We've done our duty to the elders and are off to Boodle's; would you care to accompany us? My younger brother Alexander, by the way, and our friend Mr Penn."

Thomas had been in London long enough to know that Boodle's was a gentleman's club, popular among the younger set while the older gentlemen preferred White's or Brooks, depending on their political leanings for the most part. At least they hadn't said Watier's, he mused; the infamous gamester's club was no place he cared to visit.

"Why not," he decided. When the alternative was to spend the evening here watching Ellen dance and smile with an apparently interminable series of partners presented by Lady Jersey and her cronies, spending an evening with some friendly young men of his own age sounded really quite interesting. "Pardon me a few moments while I let my aunt know

I am leaving; I can send my carriage back for her later."

"No need for that, I've my own," Danbury said cheerfully. "We'll await you in the foyer."

"Yes, yes, off you go," Lady Havers said when Thomas approached her to mention he was going to leave with some other young gentlemen. "You've done your duty to Louisa. I shall take her home when she wearies of dancing and we shall see you tomorrow."

"And Ellen."

"Excuse me?" Lady Havers blinked at him.

"Ellen. Miss Bentley, Aunt Clarice!"

"Oh, yes, of course... where is she? Sitting down with the other wallflowers?" Lady Havers spared a glance towards the side of the room. "No matter, I shall have a servant locate her when we are ready to depart."

"She is dancing; with a Major Trevithick at present, I believe."

That got Clarice's attention; her head snapped around and she stared at him. "Who introduced her to him?" she asked, her tone disbelieving. "He's one of the Earl of Exeter's sons!"

"Lady Jersey did, I believe," Thomas said, finding a perverse pleasure in the way Clarice gaped at him. "Although it might possibly have been Lady Sale, I am not sure."

"Those two interfering old biddies!" Clarice's fair expression darkened to puce. She took a deep breath, though, and forced a smile. "Well, I daresay Ellen will enjoy herself for the evening, if they have taken a momentary interest in her. They will tire of her soon enough and toss her aside."

"Indeed. I shall depend upon you, Aunt Clarice, to determine whether those they introduce her are suitable gentlemen for Ellen to associate with. A Lord Bellmere has already asked if he may call…"

"Bellmere!" Clarice's eyes fairly popped at that. "He's one of the wealthiest men in England! I tried all last season to find someone to introduce Louisa to him!"

"Well," Thomas said, "now Ellen can make the introduction for you."

For a moment he thought Clarice might slap his face, she looked so angry. He really should not prod at her so, but her unkindness to Ellen was beginning to grate on him. Making her a polite bow, he excused himself and departed to find Danbury and his cronies.

Chapter Nine

The gangling major was just escorting Ellen back to the older ladies when she spied Thomas taking his leave of their hosts. He caught her eye across the room and for a moment she thought he was going to turn away without acknowledging her, but he did nod briefly before turning away and exiting the ballroom.

"Thank you so much for asking me to dance, Major Trevithick," Ellen said. "I enjoyed our dance very much."

"I did too." The major flushed, a look rather unbecoming with his red hair, and ducked his head awkwardly. "Might I call upon you, Miss Bentley?"

"I am sure that would be acceptable," Ellen said, wondering what strange magic was about tonight, that *two* most eligible gentlemen had expressed a desire to get to know her better. "Lady Havers accepts callers on Tuesday and Friday afternoons."

"I shall look forward to it greatly," Trevithick said, "and perhaps the next time we find ourselves at the same ball, you would be so kind as to reserve me the supper dance?"

That was a singular honour indeed; Ellen's own cheeks flushed as she curtsied and said she should be delighted. The dowagers, listening avidly, beamed at her with approval and, once the major had excused himself, bombarded her with questions, demanding to know what they had talked about. Ellen hardly knew how to answer their questions; she had not thought that they talked of anything unusual. The major seemed quite shy, so after dancing a few moments in silence she had asked him if he had read any interesting books recently, hoping desperately that he was a gentleman who enjoyed reading.

"He said that he had recently re-read *Don Quixote*," Ellen told the ladies, "and I asked if he read it in translation or the original Spanish, and which translation, because I have lately read Mr Motteux's version, and rather prefer it to Mr Shelton's."

There was a brief and rather stunned silence, and then Lady Jersey laughed quite loudly. "You'll do, my girl. You'll do."

Ellen hadn't the faintest idea what Lady Jersey found so amusing. She smiled a little shyly, curtsied again and said "Perhaps it was an inappropriate conversation for me to have with a gentleman, but I am afraid I panicked a little because the major was so quiet."

"Well, some will disparagingly call you a bluestocking for it," Lady Sale said, "but let me assure you, Miss Bentley, any man worth his salt will prefer a young lady who demonstrates that she has something more than fluff between her ears."

"Oh, most certainly," Lady Jersey agreed. "A man who does not value your intelligence is not worthy of your time, my dear. Do not let anyone tell you otherwise. I despise young ladies who pretend to be something they are not to try to appeal to gentlemen, silly creatures. Getting to the altar under false pretences will not a happy marriage make."

"Who is going to the altar?" a new voice said, and Ellen felt her shoulders tighten. She forced a smile to her lips and stepped aside deferentially to allow Lady Havers to join the group.

"Nobody I know, at present," Lady Jersey said cheerfully. "About time you got your girl married off though, Clarice. Can't bring any of her suitors up to scratch, hm?"

"I'll have you know that Louisa received several offers last season," Clarice snapped.

"Oh, so she's *picky*," Lady Jersey said in enlightened tones.

Clarice's face turned red. Afraid that a full-scale confrontation was brewing, and she would be forbidden to associate the dowagers, Ellen said hastily "Aunt Clarice, I just saw Thomas, I mean Lord Havers, leaving the ball."

"Oh, don't worry about him, girl," Clarice shook her head. "He's off to sow his wild oats with some of his young friends, I daresay."

Ellen knew full well what *wild oats* referred to and she felt a knot of unhappiness lodge in her chest. Still, she made herself smile and nod. "Will we be leaving soon?" she asked, realising that she was beginning to feel very tired. It must be long past midnight, and she had not managed to break her habit of rising early in the mornings, though Clarice and Louisa were never seen until past noon.

"In a little while," Clarice looked about with a discerning eye. "Most of the eligible gentlemen have had their fill for the night and are departing. Louisa is engaged for this dance, I believe, and then I think we shall depart. Our hostess has allowed her servants to serve the wine a little too liberally and a few of the guests are becoming rowdy." She wrinkled her nose in aristocratic distaste as a young lady ran past, hotly pursued by a much older gentleman.

Ellen was shocked too, and determined that she would not accept any more dances that evening, though Mrs Peabody suggested the son of a friend who happened to be passing. "Thank you, but I have danced far more than I am accustomed to this evening," she said with a shy smile. "I should be most honoured to make your friend's acquaintance on another occasion, though."

Mrs Peabody beamed at her, and Ellen thought privately that she seemed to be a perpetually cheerful lady. She was also dressed by far the most opulently of the three dowagers, which was really saying something since all of them were in the first stare of fashion. Ellen knew little of jewels, but the multiple long strands of large, creamy pearls draped around Mrs Peabody's neck and the diamond bracelets on her wrists seemed to bespeak extreme wealth.

Louisa danced past just then on the arm of a short, rotund young man with several chins wobbling above his shirt points, and Lady Jersey snorted loudly.

"Don't think your girl will suit Ormiston, Clarice. She's not fond enough of her food!"

All three of the Dauntless Dowagers, as Ellen mentally christened them, cackled merrily at Lady Jersey's remark, and Clarice turned red again. Ellen bit back laughter too, knowing she would pay for it later if she permitted herself to be amused at Louisa's expense.

"Good evening, ladies," Clarice said frostily. "We will await the end of the dance by the stairs, Ellen." Her hand locked around Ellen's wrist like a manacle and she set off briskly, towing Ellen behind her. With no opportunity to do anything else, Ellen had to settle for bowing her head to the dowagers and saying a quick thank you for their kindnesses. They smiled benignly on her in return, so she was reassured they did not take offence at her rapid departure in Clarice's wake.

The carriage ride back to the Havers townhouse seemed endless to a weary Ellen, obliged to sit and listen to Louisa chattering excitedly about how many gentlemen had asked her to dance, and how highly titled they were. Her last partner had been a duke, about whom Clarice was particularly enthused, despite Lady Jersey's remarks.

Both the Havers ladies ignored Ellen's existence, which she had become entirely used to. They made every effort to include her in front of Thomas, Louisa going so far as to pretend they were bosom friends, but as soon as Thomas left the room the masks of civility came down.

In truth, Ellen didn't care. She had known Clarice and Louisa her entire life, had known of her relationship to them, and they had treated her as a nobody. It had taken a direct order from Thomas to even get them to acknowledge her existence, but she was quite certain they would be perfectly happy for her to disappear back into obscurity as soon as possible.

They were but a few minutes from the townhouse when Clarice at last turned her attention upon Ellen.

"And you, miss, what have you to say for yourself?"

Startled, Ellen dragged her attention away from her pensive study of the quiet, dark streets passing by outside the coach's window. "I beg your pardon, Aunt Clarice?"

"It was not well done of you at all to impose yourself upon your betters, Ellen. Why ever did you bring yourself to the notice of Lady Jersey and her friends?"

"I did not, ma'am. I was sitting quietly at the side of the room when a lady sitting in a nearby chair spoke to me. She was the one who made the introductions."

"And who was this lady?" Clarice said sharply.

"The Countess of Creighton, ma'am."

Louisa gasped at that, and Clarice's lips tightened further. "I see," she said coldly.

"Is there some reason I should not have spoken to the Countess, ma'am? She seemed perfectly respectable, and Lady Jersey and Lady Sale greeted her warmly…"

"Yes," Clarice said, "she is quite respectable. I suppose there is no reason you should have known, but Creighton was quite close to offering for Louisa at one point during her first season. He pulled back quite unexpectedly and the next thing we knew, his engagement to Miss Abingdon, as she was then, was announced."

"Well," Ellen said frankly, "I think you had a lucky escape, Cousin Louisa."

"How so?" Louisa looked quite startled.

"Lady Creighton does not appear happy in her marriage. It seems the Earl is very jealous; he does not permit her to dance with other men, nor even to speak with them if he is not present."

Louisa looked quite shocked at Ellen's revelations, looking to her mother as though asking for confirmation. Clarice shrugged a little pettishly.

"How should I have known he would behave so? Perhaps he is that way with Lady Creighton with just cause."

Both girls looked at her in confusion. Clarice pursed her lips before leaning forward and saying "Perhaps he has good reason to be jealous."

"Well, Lady Creighton is quite remarkably beautiful," Ellen said. "No doubt she will always attract attention."

Clarice sighed impatiently. "Perhaps she encourages it. Perhaps she *likes* the attention. Perhaps she even disrespects her marriage vows. It is not for us to question why the Earl of Creighton chooses to keep a close watch on his wife."

"Well," Louisa said pettishly, "I am very glad I didn't marry him after all, then. I shall certainly not give up dancing and having a good time when I marry."

Thomas would never ask you to, Ellen thought, turning her head away. *I only hope that I may find someone who will permit me my small enjoyments, too.*

Chapter Ten

Despite the lateness of the hour, Ellen could not sleep. She lay in bed gazing at the ceiling, her room well-lit by the moonlight flooding in through the open curtains. London was never quiet, and even at this hour in the exclusive streets of Belgravia she could hear the hooves of horses and the wheels of carriages outside, though more infrequently than during the daytime.

Was one of those carriages carrying Thomas home? Would he even return home? Perhaps he would spend the night at the club, with his new friends. How nice it must be, to be able to make friends and go with them on a whim, to enjoy oneself without having to answer to anyone else! Ellen had thought Lady Creighton might be a friend she could talk to, but Clarice's disapproval meant she would not be able to spend time with the lady openly. There would be no visits or outings to the shops, away from Clarice's eagle eye and Louisa's unconcealed sneers.

It was too warm in her room; with a sigh, Ellen flipped her pillow over, seeking coolness. Within five minutes her head felt hot again, though, and she sat up impatiently. She would go to the kitchen and seek a cup of milk from the pantry. Perhaps that might help her rest.

She tugged her robe on over her plain flannel nightgown. Even though her room was warm, there had been a fire blazing in there all evening to make it so, and the rest of the house would likely be quite cool. Pushing her feet into slippers, she opened her door and crept quietly to the head of the stairs.

Ellen was almost at the foot, her hand on the newel post, when the front door suddenly swung open. She froze, mouth open on a half-shriek, even though intellectually she knew Thomas must be the one coming in.

"Ellen!" Thomas seemed, if anything, more startled than she when he saw her. Placing a hand over his heart, he closed the front door, shaking his head. "You gave me a start. Whatever are you doing out of bed at this hour?"

"I could ask the same of you," she replied, feeling inexplicably argumentative. "Why is it only men who may go out to have a good time, and young ladies cannot even go to the kitchen for a cup of hot milk without being questioned?"

Typical for Thomas, he chuckled good-naturedly and came forward to offer her his arm. "A cup of hot milk sounds just the thing. Do you think we might find some bread and cheese as well? I'm starving."

Unable to stay annoyed with him, Ellen smiled. "What, do they not feed you at those fine gentlemens' clubs?"

"They have dining-rooms, I believe, but I did not see them. The gentlemen I went there with preferred to drink and gamble."

"And you?" He did not smell of strong drink, though the woodsy aroma of cigars was rising to her nose as they walked to the kitchen.

"They have very good brandy and port," Thomas admitted, "but gambling when one is in his cups is a good way to get parted from one's money. I have seen too many good men make such mistakes in America, and have no wish to fall into the same trap myself."

The kitchen was quiet, the stove banked. Ellen set her candle down on the table and headed unerringly for the pantry.

"How did you know where to find everything?" Thomas asked curiously when she set a cup of milk, half a loaf of bread, a chunk of cheese and a pat of butter wrapped in muslin in front of him.

Ellen hesitated before she took a plate from the dresser and set that down too. "Please don't tell Aunt Clarice?"

"Your secrets are safe with me, always." He smiled warmly at her, and she smiled back.

"Well, Aunt Clarice and cousin Louisa always sleep in, and sometimes I feel a little bored in the mornings, if you are gone to meet with your man of business. I asked Susan to show me the servants' areas of the house. I know about the improvements you wish to make to the servants' quarters at Haverford Hall," she continued in a babbling rush when Thomas said nothing, "but you have been dreadfully busy since we came to London and I thought you might not have had time to observe here and see if there is anything that needs to be done… I am so sorry if I have overstepped my place…"

Chuckling gently and shaking his head, Thomas held up a hand to stop her. "Ellen. Ellen! Thank you."

"Really? You don't mind?"

"I'm grateful. You must tell me what you've observed. It's obvious Aunt Clarice does not think of such things, and neither did my uncle, or the servants at Haverford would not be so ill-served. Why would things be any different here? It was something I hoped to look at in the next week or two, certainly before the cold weather begins in earnest, but I am more than happy to have your advice on the matter."

Pleased by his approval, Ellen blushed a little, casting her eyes down to the scarred, pitted surface of the scrubbed pine table. "Well—I think things are a little better here than at Haverford, in some ways. Perhaps because the house butler is not quite so intimidatingly severe as Allsopp, and for the most part the house is largely unstaffed while the family is not in residence."

Not understanding, Thomas frowned. "I don't see why that would make a difference, Ellen?"

"I talked with Dolly, the under-housekeeper," Ellen admitted. "She was just lately promoted from upstairs maid, and she talked to me about how last winter, for example, because the family did not visit, the servants were able to share all the blankets among just a few of them, rather than having to divide them between a full complement. Mr. Henry, the butler, had no objection if the blanket cupboard in the servants' area was empty, you see."

"I see," Thomas said, nodding. "This winter will be different though, won't it? Since we now have a houseful."

"Quite. And while the household budget has been increased to account for the meals the family eats, the kitchen budget for the servants has not, even though they have twice as many mouths to feed." Animated by the subject, Ellen leaned across the table to enumerate the points she wished to make, unaware that with every word she spoke, Thomas became more and more entranced by her passion.

She was, Thomas thought, quite magnificent as the words poured forth, her anger over the injustice and inequities suffered by the lower classes animating her usually still features and making her suddenly, spectacularly beautiful. She was right, too, in every point she made, and he made a mental note to have her present when he spoke with his steward, in case he forgot anything she had said.

Ellen deserved, he realised, to be mistress of a great estate. She would do far better at the task than Louisa, supposedly bred and raised for such a purpose, or any of the brainless Society misses who had been thrust under his nose thus far. How many of them would even think of the comfort of the servants who saw to their every wish? Even his aunt, herself the daughter of an earl and the mistress of a great estate for many years, did not adequately do so.

With every day Thomas spent in England, he found himself more disillusioned with the members of the aristocratic class who were supposedly his equals. The young men of his own age he had spent the evening with, while pleasant enough, thought of little beyond their own pleasures and pastimes, and the women seemed to speak of nothing but fashion and gossip. He had already decided not to take up the membership at Boodle's he had been offered, but to seek admittance to Brooks or White's instead, where the more serious business seemed to take place.

The truth was, he considered as he watched Ellen talk, her blue-grey eyes flashing in the candlelight as she spoke, her hands moving gracefully with her animation and excitement, Ellen was the only person he had met since his arrival in England with whom he really felt he had significant interests in common.

Seeming to finally notice his intent scrutiny, Ellen stopped mid-sentence before dropping her gaze and blushing. "I am so sorry, here I am rattling on and you must be exhausted!"

"Not at all," Thomas said firmly. "I am just thinking, though, that I may not remember tomorrow—later today, that is—everything you are saying. Can I ask you to attend the meeting I have scheduled with my steward at two this afternoon? He can take notes and we can discuss how best to address the issues you have observed."

Ellen looked delighted to be asked, but she wrinkled her nose and tapped her finger on her lower lip. "We are supposed to be at home to callers this afternoon—though I daresay Aunt Clarice and Louisa will hardly notice if I am not present. I am sure I can slip away."

"Absolutely," Thomas agreed. "I shall see you at two, then. Now off to bed with you, and get some rest." He tempered the order with a warm smile, and she flashed one of her own in return.

"Good night, Thomas," her voice floated across the darkened kitchen as she left him alone, and for a long time Thomas sat in silence, lost in thought.

Chapter Eleven

As Ellen had expected, even before the clock struck two, Mr. Henry was admitting the first of a stream of gentlemen callers eager to pay court to Louisa. None of them gave her a second glance, and when she quietly whispered a request to be excused to her aunt a few minutes later, Clarice didn't even look at her before waving her hand in dismissal.

The study door stood open, and Thomas looked up with a smile of welcome when she hesitated outside, wondering if she should knock. "Ellen! Come on in. Please, allow me to introduce my steward, Mr. Gallagher."

Ellen froze for a moment, unsure whether she should curtsy. The steward offered a deep bow, she decided not, and settled for a little dip of her head. "A pleasure to make your acquaintance, sir."

"The honour is mine, Miss Bentley. Please, Lord Havers has been telling me that you have assessed the servants' quarters here and have some recommendations?"

Pleased by the businesslike way he addressed her, Ellen accepted the chair Thomas held for her to sit, and soon the three of them had their heads together over a thick sheaf of papers, Mr. Gallagher taking copious notes.

"Excuse me, my lord," Mr. Henry interrupted them about a quarter hour later. "Lady Havers is requesting Miss Bentley's presence in the Chinese Drawing Room."

Thomas looked up with a frown. "Why?" he asked bluntly.

Mr. Henry coughed delicately. "Two of the callers who are lately arrived, are here specifically to see Miss Bentley, my lord." He paused. "They have brought flowers."

Thomas was on his feet before he knew what he was about. "Gentlemen callers for Ellen—I mean Miss Bentley? Who are they?" he rapped out.

It was only after he had spoken that it occurred to him, he did not care a whit who had come to call for Louisa.

"Lord Bellmere and Major Trevithick, my lord," Mr. Henry answered him with a hint of something in his expression that might have been approval. The staff appreciated his concern for Ellen's welfare, he supposed; after all, she showed concern for theirs. They would want to see her happy and well settled.

"I shall escort you, Ellen," Thomas decided. "I think we've left Gallagher enough to be going on with for now, hm?"

"Indeed, my lord, I shall get to work straight away," the steward agreed.

"Shall we?" Thomas invited, offering his arm for Ellen. She looked at him queerly.

"I thought you did not care for Aunt Clarice's At Homes?" she queried softly as they left the study.

"I wished for a break," he fibbed smoothly, "and some of Cook's delicious lemon tarts, which I happen to know she made this morning. And, of course, to meet your suitors, Ellen."

"They are not my suitors," Ellen said at once, too quickly for Thomas' liking.

The lady doth protest too much, he thought as he watched the blush colour her cheeks. Did she already have a preference for one of the gentlemen, after a single evening in his company? Silently, he cursed himself for leaving the ball last night. Clearly, one or other of the two men had taken the opportunity to get to know Ellen, and had made a favourable impression.

The Chinese Drawing Room was packed to capacity, it seemed, as Mr. Henry opened the door for them with a bow. Faces turned in their direction, mostly gentlemen though a few had brought their mothers and sisters along. Several female faces brightened notably at the sight of Thomas, but he ignored them all, watching with narrowed eyes as two gentlemen approached with broad smiles.

"Cousin, pray allow me to introduce Lord Bellmere and Major Trevithick," Ellen made the introductions. "My cousin, Lord Havers."

Both men bowed with the perfect amount of deference to a peer of his rank, but it was more than clear that their interest was fixed upon Ellen. Neither of them seemed a brainless fribble blithering out fulsome compliments, either, rather to Thomas' irritation. Indeed, both seemed intelligent, thoughtful gentlemen of exactly the sort he would rather like to know better… if they weren't making calf eyes at Ellen.

"I met with my cousin on the board of the Museum this morning," Bellmere was telling Ellen genially. "The Museum is closed to the general public until noon on Mondays and Tuesdays, so if an early morning outing would be acceptable, I should be delighted to escort you to see the Elgin Marbles."

Ellen looked quite delighted too, though she very properly said "I should have to seek Lady Havers' permission, of course, and arrange for a chaperone…"

"No need to bother Aunt Clarice," Thomas said jovially. "I should like to see the Marbles too. I can chaperone you."

"Perhaps we might make a party of it," Major Trevithick said, and Thomas thought he would have to watch out for the military man. Likely a master of strategy, Trevithick could well sneak into Ellen's favour right under both his and Bellmere's noses.

"Did you say a party? Are we giving a party, cousin?" Louisa called from across the room, obviously put out that they were having a conversation of which she was not the central focus.

Left with no choice but to include Louisa, Thomas took a few reluctant steps closer to inform her of Lord Bellmere's proposed outing to the Museum. He was astonished when Louisa claimed a great interest in being one of the party, but did not take long to discern her reasoning. Lord Bellmere was reputed to be one of the wealthiest men in England, after all, and Louisa was piqued that the baronet had not chosen to join the ranks of her suitors, but instead expressed an interest in Ellen.

With Louisa's avowal of interest, suddenly all her suitors expressed a great desire to view Lord Elgin's famous acquisitions too, and Bellmere acquired a distinctly aggrieved look, though he was gentleman enough to promise they might all attend.

Thomas caught a slight smirk playing around Major Trevithick's lips as Bellmere was drawn inexorably into the circle around Louisa. Turning away as though disinterested, the major picked up a book lying on a side table and asked Ellen a question about it which Thomas did not hear, as he was addressed at that moment by an older lady seeking to bring her daughter to his notice.

Louisa's tinkling laugh rang out, and Thomas glanced across to see her lay a hand on Bellmere's sleeve, smiling coyly up at him.

It hit him then, all of a sudden.

He did not care in the slightest who Louisa smiled at or flirted with, despite having been briefly bowled over by her beauty. He cared very much, though, that Ellen had her head bowed over a book with Major Trevithick, a small smile playing about her soft lips.

Jealousy was an entirely new emotion for Thomas, and he found he did not care for the feeling at all. *He* wanted to be the only one favoured with Ellen's smiles.

In the centre of a crowded drawing-room was probably the worst possible place for his true feelings to suddenly become clear, Thomas realised, but there was nothing he could do about the fact that his entire world had just turned topsy-turvy.

Clarice was looking at him strangely, coming across to intercept the persistent woman with the daughter and remove Thomas to Louisa's side, which she obviously felt was his proper place. Clarice was going to be disappointed, Thomas thought dimly, but he knew now he could never marry Louisa, even if her feelings for him were what Clarice claimed. His minor infatuation with her beauty was as nothing compared to what he felt for Ellen.

Love. He whispered the word silently, inside the vaults of his own mind, and knew it for an immutable, timeless truth. He loved Ellen; loved everything about her, from her intelligent, curious mind to her kindness and empathy for others. Best of all, she would be the kind of Countess he had imagined ever since his grandfather's stories of Havers when he was a child; a gracious lady of the manor, always aware of the needs of her people.

Ellen glanced up from the book just then, looking around the room until her gaze settled on Thomas. At once she smiled, more widely than the slight smile she had given the major. Thomas smiled back, wishing everyone else in the room to perdition so he could tell Ellen how he felt—but no, he must not rush this. She had not the slightest idea, he thought, and he had thus far encouraged her to treat him as a trusted older brother. What a fool he was! He should have recognised her sterling qualities earlier, realised that his delight in her company was far more than mere friendship. Now he would have to fight off other suitors for her hand, all while convincing Ellen his intentions were genuine… and somehow not allowing Clarice or Louisa to figure out what he was about, lest they sabotage his suit.

At that moment, Thomas rather wished he could plead a headache and quit the room. But no; he would not leave the field to Trevithick and Bellmere, who had slipped from Louisa's court back to Ellen's side, insinuating himself into her conversation with the major.

The At Home seemed to last forever. Thomas was sure a half-hour was considered the polite maximum of time to spend at such things before taking one's leave, and indeed most of Louisa's court seemed to drift in and out, though there was always a constant circle around her. Neither Lord Bellmere nor Major Trevithick showed any inclination to depart, however, eyeing one another like a pair of wary cats. Ellen did not seem to favour either of them above the other, which was some comfort at least to Thomas. She merely seemed delighted to have someone willing to make intelligent conversation with her.

Clarice watched from across the room with sharp eyes as Thomas remained at Ellen's side, and no sooner had the last of their guests finally departed than she was ordering the two girls upstairs to dress for dinner and catching Thomas' arm.

"You must not hover so over Ellen, nephew. Louisa felt quite neglected! It was very ill-done of

Ellen to monopolise Lord Bellmere and Major Trevithick, too!"

"Ellen is in her first season, ma'am," Thomas said reasonably. "While Louisa is in her third, quite comfortable handling a horde of enthusiastic swains. I did not observe her to be forlorn. Quite the opposite, actually." Louisa had laughed often and loudly, though Thomas caught her sneaking regular looks at their little grouping. "If anything distressed her, it was undoubtedly that she was not the centre of everyone's attention, for once."

"Thomas!" Clarice affected shock. "That is unkind!"

"It is the truth," Thomas said curtly. "Two dukes, a marquis and any number of earls, barons and heirs danced attendance on your daughter this afternoon, Aunt Clarice. Louisa should not grudge Ellen a pair of suitors who are discerning enough to see her good qualities."

Clarice's mouth flattened to a thin line. "Good qualities?" she said scornfully. "She is a parson's daughter with little in the way of manners and no looks to recommend her! You waste your time and diminish the family name with your recognition of her!"

Shocked, Thomas stared at her. "Ellen Bentley is my relative by blood," he said, his tone quiet but with a dangerous edge to it. "She has more right to my time, and to the family name, than you do. Indeed, I have no doubt that she will—*would* make a far better Countess than you have ever been!"

His slip of the tongue did not go unnoticed. Eyes narrowed, Clarice spat out "Oh, I see how it is. The hussy has seduced you, right underneath Louisa's nose!"

"That will be quite enough," Thomas said, surprising himself with the snap in his voice. "You will keep a civil tongue in your head when you speak of Ellen, or you will find yourself no longer welcome beneath my roof."

If looks could kill, he would no doubt have been struck dead on the spot. "Upstart American," Clarice hissed. "You understand nothing of class and society!"

"I understand I want nothing to do with any society which cannot recognise the superior qualities of an intelligent young woman with a kind heart, merely because she is three generations removed from an earldom rather than one!"

They were both breathing fast, voices raised. Clarice looked away first, though, when she saw Thomas clearly had no intention of backing down.

"I am only thinking of Louisa's future," she muttered.

"As you should," Thomas said, gentling his tone. "There are, however, many eligible suitors for Louisa's hand. This is her third season, Aunt, and I do not doubt that she has been just as overwhelmed with suitors throughout the previous two. What is she waiting for?"

Clarice hesitated before sighing heavily. "I do not know," she admitted. "She seems to delight in having every man at her feet; if she chooses one, I think she fears the others will all abandon her."

"That is rather the point of a marriage," Thomas said, not unkindly. "I should not want a wife who wanted to be surrounded and adored by other suitors."

"Of course not."

Clarice's head was down, and Thomas realised his aunt was deeply distressed about something. Gently, he took her arm and guided her to a chaise, pressing her to take a seat.

"Is there something you want to tell me, Aunt?" he asked gently.

There were tears on her cheeks when she looked up at him. "Perhaps we spoiled her," Clarice said, her voice cracking. "Yet I too was a little spoiled by my parents, and I am sure I was not so awful as Louisa can be when she does not get her way. I saw her face when Lord Bellmere left her to return to Ellen, and you followed; someone will pay for that, Thomas."

"What do you mean?" He really didn't understand.

Clarice hesitated before the words spilled from her in a rush. "She is my daughter, the only child I have left, but God help me, she terrifies me! She stabbed a maid once with a pair of scissors; the poor girl almost bled to death, Havers had to pay her off…"

Thomas' jaw dropped. He could scarcely believe what his aunt was saying. "Louisa stabbed a maid?" he said faintly as Clarice sobbed.

"There was so much blood," Clarice sniffled. "And Louisa seemed so calm, just stabbing her again and again, saying that Nellie had made eyes at Mr Danvers while she was carrying in the tea tray."

"Christ!" Thomas was appalled. There was something seriously wrong with Louisa, that was obvious. He'd thought Clarice's efforts to satisfy

Louisa's every whim were just those of a mother over-indulging a spoiled daughter, but now he realised Clarice was terrified of the consequences should Louisa feel she was not receiving her due.

"Oh, dear God. *Ellen.*"

He was on his feet without conscious thought, running for the door, sprinting across the hall to take the stairs three at a time, shouting Ellen's name.

Behind him, he heard Clarice call his name, but he ignored her entirely, too focused on getting to Ellen as quickly as possible. Just in case. Surely Louisa wouldn't hurt her, but…

He ran faster.

Chapter Twelve

"What a delightful afternoon!" Louisa exclaimed as they walked up the stairs together. "Did you enjoy yourself, Ellen?"

"I did, yes," Ellen agreed.

"Were you surprised to receive callers yourself? You looked surprised, when you entered the parlour to see Major Trevithick and Lord Bellmere."

"I was," Ellen admitted. "Though both of them asked at the ball last night if they might call on me, I confess I did not truly expect them to do so, and certainly not so soon."

Louisa hummed to herself and nodded. "Come into my room so we can talk further," she invited as they reached her door. "I've had two seasons already, and my fair share of importunate suitors. There are things you should know."

Her last words were delivered with a tone and expression of dire warning. Concerned, Ellen immediately followed Louisa into her room, where Louisa's maid looked up in consternation from her task of laying out clean clothes on the bed.

"M'lady?"

'Leave us," Louisa said, waving a hand towards the door. "I'll ring when I need you."

"Very good, m'lady!" The girl scurried quickly from the room, closing the door behind her.

Louisa wandered over to the bed, hummed thoughtfully as she inspected the gown laid out there, and turned away, crossing the room to an elegant writing-desk by the window.

Uncertain what she should do, Ellen stood close to the door, waiting for Louisa to speak, or invite her to a chair. After a couple of minutes of silence, though, she spoke first.

"What sort of things do you think I should know, cousin?"

Louisa did not speak for another full minute, toying with an ornate silver letter-opener on her desk, before turning and looking at Ellen. "Which of them will you choose?" she asked.

Confused, Ellen blinked. "Excuse me?"

"Major Trevithick, or Lord Bellmere. Which will you choose? You are unlikely to find any other suitors, you know. Best for you to accept one of them quickly, before they come to realise you are not truly of our station. Look how Thomas hovered close when you spoke with them today, terrified you would say or do something to embarrass the Havers name."

Horrified, Ellen took a step back as Louisa approached her. "Really?" Her voice shook. "I did not think…"

Louisa sneered. "Why else would he leave my side, for *you*?"

Ellen's head drooped forward. She had no answer for that question; Thomas' admiration for Louisa had been evident from the first time she saw them together. With a crowd of rival suitors in the room, surely Thomas would not have left Louisa's side unless he saw a clear duty to do so.

"So I ask again, which shall it be, Trevithick or Bellmere?" Louisa pressed.

"I barely know either of them! Why do you demand I choose now? Surely it is not so urgent!" *I could not possibly make a decision of such magnitude on such a slight acquaintance*, Ellen thought with a surge of anger.

Louisa's beautiful face twisted with a sudden rage. "I was willing to allow you one," she said, her voice a low, harsh snarl. "Mama said I must let you have one. You're being greedy, Ellen." She changed to a high, almost sing-song voice. "Choose, Ellen, you have to choose!"

Louisa was making no sense, and acting very strangely. Suddenly frightened, Ellen took another step back, towards the door.

A clawlike hand locked around her wrist. "You have to choose, Ellen. You're being naughty."

"Let go of me," Ellen said, trying to keep her tone steady even though panic gripped at her insides, making her knees tremble. "You're hurting my wrist. Thomas will be angry with you for hurting me."

Louisa tilted her head to one side, and a dreadful rictus of a grin spread across her beautiful face. "I know your *seeeeeecret*," she said, drawing the word out. "So foolish, to think Thomas would ever look at you. Such a silly, naive little girl."

Ellen swallowed. "Let go of me," she said again, but it was becoming harder to speak calmly. Louisa's grip was tight, and despite her fragile appearance, the other girl was terrifyingly strong. "You're not well, Louisa." Indeed, she was beginning to fear that her cousin was not entirely sane. There was a strange light in Louisa's blue eyes that spoke of madness.

"Enough!" Louisa shouted suddenly. "You won't *listen*!"

Ellen gasped as Louisa's other hand came up between them, silver flashing as she brought the letter-opener from her writing-desk to Ellen's throat.

"Louisa, don't," she croaked, suddenly petrified.

"You won't listen, so I have to make you be quiet," Louisa crooned. Cold metal traced over Ellen's skin, pressing lightly at first, and then harder. Frightened to breathe, wondering just how sharp the letter-opener was, Ellen stood stock still.

"I knew you'd ruin everything from the moment Thomas insisted you come to live at the Hall. You should have married some yeoman farmer and stayed in the country. Then I wouldn't have to do *this*."

Louisa was going to kill her, Ellen realised incredulously. She was insane, and she was actually going to kill Ellen.

Some ancient instinct of self-defence kicked in as Louisa drew back her arm, and Ellen jumped back, her free hand coming up to try and fend Louisa off. The other girl was still holding onto her wrist, though, and Ellen couldn't get free. Her heel caught on the edge of one of the floor rugs and she tripped, falling backwards. Landing with a thud, she finally managed to get out a scream as Louisa came down atop her, malevolence written all over her beautiful features as she stabbed the knife down.

Unable to escape, it was all Ellen could do to try and swipe Louisa's arm aside with her own. Instead of piercing her heart, the knife caught her forearm instead, driving clean between the delicate bones of her wrist and piercing deep into the floorboards with the force of the thrust.

Ellen screamed with shock at the excruciating pain, pinned to the floor by the knife through her arm.

"Damn you!" Louisa shouted, yanking at the knife, but it was stuck fast. Ellen screamed again, agonised, as the knife shifted slightly inside her arm. "Damn you, just *die*!" Letting go of the knife, she put her hands around Ellen's neck and squeezed.

"Ellen!" Thomas roared her name, cursing his legs for not carrying him faster as he took the stairs three at a time, suddenly absolutely certain that Ellen was in mortal danger. "*Ellen!*" He flung her bedroom door open without bothering to knock, startling her poor maid. "Where is she, Susan?"

Susan just shook her head, staring at him with wide eyes, and Thomas spun on his heel. If Ellen hadn't made it to her room, she must have gone into Louisa's for some reason. Louisa had lured her in, undoubtedly, and Ellen, in her innocence of Louisa's true nature, had trusted her.

A scream of pure terror made his heart clench, and he never afterwards remembered the steps which took him the length of the hallway to Louisa's suite.

The sight which greeted him as he flung Louisa's door wide would stay with him forever; Ellen on her back on the floor, blood spreading in a wide pool from her arm, pinned to the floorboards by a gleaming silver knife. Louisa knelt atop her still form, her hands around Ellen's throat.

Ellen's face was blue.

Louisa looked up at him, her mouth opening, but what she would have said would have to remain unknown. Thomas had never in his life struck a woman, but he didn't think twice before grabbing Louisa by the shoulders and throwing her bodily across the room.

Falling to his knees beside Ellen's still body, Thomas cried out her name in utter despair.

"Thomas," Clarice said from the doorway, and then as she took in the scene, "Oh, dear God in Heaven."

"It is all her fault!" Louisa cried from across the room, where she had fallen when Thomas flung her off Ellen. "She would not choose!"

"What have you done?" Clarice cried, utterly distraught. "Oh, Louisa, what have you *done*?"

"My lord?"

Thomas glanced up to find his valet Kenneth at the head of a crowd of servants, all with shocked expressions on their faces.

"Send for a doctor," he ordered, "and take her," he pointed a shaking finger at Louisa, "and lock her up somewhere until I can find a magistrate."

Clarice set up a terrible wail, but Thomas had no time for her. The danger of Louisa dealt with, he turned his attention back to Ellen. She was terribly still, but the blue colour was fading slightly from her face, giving him hope that she might yet live. Leaning down close to her face, he turned his head to the side, hoping to feel her breath upon his cheek.

There; the faintest whisper of air! "She lives," he gasped in relief.

"Miss Ellen!" Susan shrieked as she pushed her way through the crowd of shocked, whispering servants and fell to her knees on the other side of Ellen's body. "Oh, Miss Ellen! Whatever *happened?*"

Thomas couldn't answer her, only shaking his head as Kenneth manhandled a strangely silent Louisa from the room with the aid of a burly footman. He could hear Mr Henry issuing orders, sending several footmen running to find a doctor as fast as possible, but everything seemed very far away as he knelt beside Ellen's still form, placing his hand gently against her pale cheek.

"M'lord," he looked up as Susan spoke loudly. The maid was pale, but her hands were steady as she reached out to him imploringly. "M'lord… if we wait until the doctor gets here, it might be too late."

Thomas frowned, not sure what she meant, at least until she pointed to the steadily spreading pool of blood beneath Ellen's arm.

"We have to stop the bleeding, m'lord, or she might bleed to death before they find a doctor." Reaching behind her to untie the strings of her apron, Susan nodded at him. "I can bandage her arm with this, for now, if you will pull out the knife."

Thomas felt queasy at the mere idea, but Susan was quite right, and at least Ellen seemed to be unconscious, so hopefully she would feel no pain. Taking a deep breath, he grasped the hilt of the knife, trying not to think about the force with which Louisa must have stabbed Ellen, to have the knife go right through her arm and jam in the floor.

Not wanting to wiggle the knife about and maybe do more damage, he gave it a single, sharp yank with all his might. The knife popped free and he threw it aside, unable to bear touching it for a moment longer than necessary.

"Hold this," Susan said, handing him one of the apron strings. Grateful that she seemed to know what to do, Thomas obeyed, watching as she wrapped the folded cloth tightly around Ellen's arm, covering both cuts. Tying the strings off once she had finished, she sat back on her heels and bit her lip nervously. "Perhaps you should move her to the bed, m'lord?"

"Not in here." Thomas didn't want Ellen to wake up in Louisa's room. "Her own room." A little colour was returning to Ellen's pale cheeks, though he could see purpling bruises springing up on her throat. Gently, he gathered her in his arms, giving Susan a grateful smile when she carefully lifted Ellen's injured arm and placed her hand across her stomach. The maid hurried ahead of him, urging other shocked servants out of their way and holding doors open wide, pulling back the covers on Ellen's bed as Thomas prepared to lay her down.

"Thank you," Thomas said as Susan removed Ellen's shoes. He should leave, he supposed, particularly as the housekeeper came bustling in then with several more maids, but he couldn't bear to let Ellen out of his sight.

"Anything for Miss Bentley, m'lord. She's been right kind to me." Susan sniffled slightly, but Thomas did not comment on the tears rolling down her cheeks.

"She'll be fine," he said bracingly, as much to himself as Susan. "She's strong. And we'll take good care of her, won't we?"

"The best, m'lord," Susan said fervently. "The very best."

Chapter Thirteen

The doctor seemed to take forever to come. The housekeeper tried to shoo Thomas out, but he refused to leave Ellen's side, afraid she might perish if for even a moment he took his eyes from the faint rise and fall of her chest. The white apron bandage wrapped tightly around her arm was slowly turning crimson with blood. How much had she already lost? How much could a person lose, and live? Would the doctor be able to close the wounds properly? Sitting beside Ellen on her bed, her hand clasped in his, Thomas bowed his head and prayed that Ellen would recover.

"The doctor is here, m'lord," Mr Henry said from the doorway, and Thomas lifted his head to see a small, grey-haired man wearing a slightly threadbare suit and thick glasses.

"Doctor Smithee, at your service, m'lord."

Thomas appreciated that the doctor didn't waste time bowing and scraping, but came briskly forward, stopping at the bedside and eyeing him. "It's probably best if you leave the room, m'lord. No doubt your staff can amply assist me."

"I'm not going anywhere," Thomas said firmly. "Miss Bentley is my ward, and my responsibility." And the guilt was his too, he acknowledged privately; he would always blame himself for not pressing Clarice earlier, discovering Louisa's predilection for violence. He'd trusted blindly and put Ellen in danger because of it.

Dr Smithee seemed to accept his pronouncement and moved around to the other side of the bed, displacing Susan who stood wringing her hands while the doctor examined Ellen's neck, humming quietly under his breath. Someone had obviously informed him of the situation before showing him into the room, for which Thomas was grateful.

"Nasty," Smithee said finally, "but the bruising is not so severe as to put her life at risk, I believe.

Cool compresses of water and witch hazel will be beneficial."

The housekeeper sent a maid scurrying from the room at once, and the doctor turned his attention to Ellen's arm.

"Quick thinking, to bandage it so tightly," he said approvingly. "Your handiwork, m'lord?"

"I cannot take credit; it was Miss Bentley's maid, Susan, who suggested we stop the bleeding and used her apron as a bandage," Thomas nodded towards Susan, who blushed and ducked her head.

"Good work, girl. I don't suppose you'd be interested in a career change? Good nurses with common sense like yours are hard to find."

Susan looked quite startled, but shook her head emphatically. "I'm happy being a ladies' maid, sir," she said shyly. "I shouldn't want to leave Miss Bentley, besides."

"No doubt she will be glad of your service. Now, let's have a look here. A narrow blade, hm?" The doctor peered closely at the wound on the upper side of Ellen's arm as he uncovered it.

"It was a letter-opener, I believe," Thomas said bleakly, thinking even as he spoke that Louisa must have secretly sharpened the blade, making sure she always had a lethal weapon on hand. Whatever was he do with her? Perhaps he should ask the good doctor's advice, after Ellen had been taken care of.

By the time Dr Smithee had finished putting several stitches in each side of Ellen's arm, the other maid had returned with a basin of clean water mixed with witch hazel. The doctor took one of the clean cloths the maid proffered and soaked it in the water, squeezing it out before placing it carefully across the bruises on Ellen's throat.

"Change the cloth every half hour," the doctor instructed Susan. "Now, let us see if we cannot bring Miss Bentley back to her senses, hm?" Removing a small vial from his bag, he uncapped it and held it under Ellen's nose.

The strong scent of sal ammoniac made Thomas' eyes water, and it seemed to work even on Ellen in her unconscious state, because her eyelids fluttered and she coughed.

"Ellen," Thomas said urgently, squeezing her hand. "Ellen! Open your eyes, dearest."

Her eyelids fluttered again, and he realised inconsequentially that he had never noticed how long and dark her lashes were, a thick fan brushing the paleness of her cheek.

"Tho-Thomas?" she whispered thickly, before coughing again. "Uh." She tried to lift her hand towards her throat, but he squeezed her fingers gently.

"Don't try to talk, dearest. Your throat is very bruised." Gazing at her, he tried to smile reassuringly as she opened her eyes fully at last, looking directly at him.

"I feel so tired," Ellen whispered, and her lashes drifted down again. Panicking, Thomas looked at the doctor, who nodded reassuringly.

"After blood loss like that, she will be weary for some time. Beef tea every day will soon see her right, though of course you must watch carefully for infection."

Thomas listened carefully as the doctor spoke, outlining what must be done for Ellen's care. He promised to attend every day to check on her until she was entirely recovered from her ordeal, too.

"I wonder if I might speak to you regarding the, ah, perpetrator?" Thomas said quietly as Dr Smithee began to pack his things away in his bag again. He did not wish to leave Ellen, but gently laid her hand down and eased off the bed, moving over to the window and beckoning the doctor to join him.

"I take it someone told you who attacked Ellen?" Thomas asked softly.

"Indeed." The doctor peered at him over his spectacles. "Forgive me for saying so, my lord, but it sounds as though Lady Louisa may be somewhat, ah, *disturbed*."

"I trust we can rely on your discretion in the matter? I will make it worth your while."

Dr Smithee looked properly horrified. "Of course, my lord! My patients' confidentiality is of the utmost importance!"

He wouldn't be a doctor to the aristocracy otherwise, Thomas supposed. Word would soon spread of his inability to keep secrets.

"That's good," he said aloud. "My aunt has made me aware that this is not Lady Louisa's first episode of violence. She came horrifyingly close to killing Miss Bentley today, and it is obvious to me that she must be withdrawn from society and treated for her illness. I was wondering if you had any recommendations?"

Smithee squinted a little and sucked on his teeth. "I understand you are an American, my lord— have you perhaps heard of the Bethlem Hospital?"

"Bedlam, you mean? I have, but surely such a remedy is entirely unsuitable for a young lady such as my cousin, however disturbed her mind!" Thomas had read of the infamous hospital for the insane in the newspapers, and indeed going to tour the facility had been suggested to him, though he could think of nothing more grotesque.

"Indeed, I should never recommend such a place. Bethlem is the most famous, but there are several treatment facilities for those of unsound mind, both in London and in the countryside. A friend of mine I attended medical school with is the senior psychiatrist in residence at a small facility on the Isle of Wight. They accept only a few patients from the upper classes at a time, who are looked after very well, of course. Perhaps I should write him a letter and enquire whether they might have a vacancy?"

"Thank you," Thomas said gratefully. "We shall be leaving London as soon as Ellen—Miss Bentley, that is—is fit to travel, and I should hope to have somewhere to take Lady Louisa before that."

Ellen coughed from the bed, and Thomas turned away from the doctor immediately, eager to return to her. Though he knew Louisa would have to be dealt with—and he would have to talk seriously with Clarice, too—right now, he couldn't bear to be away from Ellen's side.

Susan, however, seemed to have other ideas. Intercepting him before he reached the bed, the maid

161

curtsied deferentially before saying "Begging your pardon, m'lord, but we need to make Miss Bentley comfortable."

Thomas frowned, looking at Ellen reclining against her pillows. She looked perfectly comfortable to him.

"Get that dress off her and settle her into bed," Susan said more bluntly, and he nodded, finally understanding. Ellen's dress was blood-spattered and stained, and she would surely be distressed if she woke to find herself still wearing it.

"I should go and check on my aunt, and ensure Lady Louisa is safely confined," Thomas suggested, and Susan gave him an approving nod and another curtsy.

Ellen woke with a throbbing ache in her arm and a desperate thirst. Coughing hurt, a great deal, until a strong arm behind her shoulders pushed her up to a sitting position and a glass was held to her lips.

Water dribbled into her mouth, soothing and cool, flavoured lightly with honey and lemon. She swallowed, coughed, sipped a little more.

"Easy," Thomas' voice said quietly into her ear. "Drink slowly."

"Thomas?" Exhausted by the effort of drinking, she whispered his name as her head rolled back against his shoulder. An unseen hand took the glass away, and Thomas guided her gently to lie down again. "What happened?" Her voice was a thin thread, every word a huge effort to push out.

"Louisa attacked you."

All at once, Ellen remembered. Her whole body stiffened, her eyes flying wide open as she jerked, trying to sit up.

"It's all right," Thomas soothed, gently pressing her back down. "She can't hurt you. You're quite safe."

It really hurt too much to speak, but Ellen lifted her arm to look at the bandage swathing her arm. She hadn't imagined it, then, the dreadful pain as Louisa's knife stabbed through her flesh.

"Ellen," Thomas said, and she raised her eyes to look at him. He sat close beside the bed in a chair, his coat cast aside, shirtsleeves rolled up to reveal tanned forearms. He looked haggard, and for the first time she could recall, there was no smile on his handsome face for her. "Oh Ellen, I'm so sorry."

She shook her head at him, forced out a few words. "Not your fault."

"Clarice confessed Louisa has been violent before. She attacked a maid, once; stabbed her with a pair of scissors for supposedly making eyes at one of her suitors. She seems to need to be the centre of attention, and once Clarice admitted that, I realised her jealousy towards you might have turned more sinister."

How could he ever have known Louisa might snap like that, though? Ellen shook her head at him again, reaching out to touch his cheek as his head lowered, though she winced as she moved her arm.

"*Not* your fault," she whispered again.

"You'll never have to see her again. I promise you that. Mr Gallagher is looking into a hospital for the disturbed of mind, which the doctor who saw you suggested."

"Not Bedlam!" Ellen's eyes widened again.

"No, not Bedlam. A place on the Isle of Wight, I understand. A country house, a place where Louisa can rest and be treated for whatever sickness of the mind makes her act so."

Silent, Ellen watched Thomas. *He must be devastated*, she thought. "And when she is better?" she whispered finally. "Will you marry her?"

Thomas' head snapped up, his expression pure shock. "Marry Louisa?" he exclaimed. "Good God, no! How could Louisa ever be permitted to marry *anyone*? What if she had *children*, Ellen?"

"You think the madness might be passed on?"

"That, or she might be a danger to them herself! I could never forgive myself if she harmed a child, knowing I had it in my power to ensure she would never have the chance. No," Thomas shook his head. "Should any man ask to marry Louisa, I would be compelled to tell them the truth."

No man would marry Louisa then, Ellen knew. Or if one did, it would be solely for her dowry, and he would likely do something awful like shut her up in Bedlam. At least in refusing her the chance to marry, Thomas protected her from that.

"I'm so sorry," she whispered. "You must be devastated. I know you loved her."

Chapter Fourteen

Thomas blinked in surprise as Ellen whispered her sympathetic words, her delicate hand outstretched to touch lightly on his wrist.

"You think I'm in love with *Louisa*," he said, in dawning realisation. "I am most assuredly not, Ellen."

Her sidelong look expressed cynicism at his denial.

"Really! Yes, I was somewhat blinded by her beauty at first, but it did not take me long to recognise she and I have absolutely no interests in common. Every time we try to talk, it ends in uncomfortable silence as I run out of things to say to her."

Ellen's lips twitched. She did not think she had ever even seen Thomas reduced to an uncomfortable silence; he never seemed to have any issues talking to *her*.

Seeing her amusement, Thomas lifted her hand to his lips, pressing a kiss against the back of it gently. "It has taken me a quite unconscionably long time, however, to realise I have already met the only woman with whom I *can* imagine spending the rest of my life in perfect harmony and contentment."

Ellen's brow furrowed as she obviously wondered who he meant, causing Thomas to shake his head and laugh. She was too modest.

"You, Ellen," he said gently. "I mean you."

Her eyes widened, lips parting with shock. She did not attempt to speak, though, so he ploughed valiantly on, hoping desperately that she would not reject him without thinking it over, at least.

"From our very first meeting, I was struck by your kindness and your good nature; the way you treat others, especially servants, sets an example I wish more would follow. It is to my shame that I did not comprehend until now, when two other men saw at first sight your eminent good qualities and immediately desired to court you, just how empty my life would be if you married another. I love you, Ellen. I cannot imagine living my life without seeing you every day, without talking to you about the issues which trouble me, sharing with you my triumphs and tragedies."

Ellen's eyes welled with tears as she gazed at him, but still she did not speak. Thomas stumbled on.

"When I saw you lying on the floor with blood everywhere, my heart stopped. I would have done anything in that moment, given even my own life, for you to just look at me and smile."

She smiled at him as a tear trickled down her cheek. Reaching to stroke it away gently, he begged "Forgive me for being slow to come to the understanding there is nobody else I could possibly love." Hesitating briefly, he plunged on. "This may be the most inopportune moment I could possibly have chosen but... I love you quite desperately, you see, and if I do not ask you to marry me now, I may never pluck up the courage."

Ellen could scarcely believe what Thomas was saying. It was every wistful daydream she ever had, all coming true at once. The only problem was that she could barely make a sound.

"Ask me again once I can speak," she whispered through happy tears, "so that I may fully express all the joy I feel at this moment."

At once, Thomas' expression of trepidation changed to pure joy, and he lifted her hand to his mouth again and lavished kisses upon it. "Dearest love," he said, over and over again, "my dearest, darling Ellen!"

She still wondered if she was in some sort of fever dream, but if it truly was a dream, she would be quite happy never to awaken. Thomas took out his handkerchief and dried her wet face before leaning in to press a respectful kiss on her cheek. Which did more than anything else to convince her it was real; surely if it was a dream, he would have been a little less respectful and addressed her lips, as she had daydreamed of so many times.

It was only then, when Thomas stood up and said she should rest, that he had to speak with Clarice, that Ellen realised they had never been alone. Susan had been sitting on a stool at the end of the bed the whole time.

"Are you hungry, Miss? The doctor recommended beef broth for you and I have some warm here, if you think you could sip a little," Susan said, as Thomas departed the room.

Blushing furiously, Ellen nodded.

Susan smiled shyly at her as she came to stand at her side. "It isn't my place to say, really, Miss, but congratulations," the maid said, smiling broadly. "You and m'lord will be very happy together, I am sure! All the staff will be overjoyed to hear the news you are to be their new mistress!"

That was something she hadn't even considered; in marrying Thomas, she would become the new Countess of Havers, which was a rather nerve-wracking proposition. She was reassured, however, that Thomas would not wish her to ape Clarice, with her haughty ways and dismissal of those who did not share her exalted rank.

Susan helped Ellen sip warm beef broth from a small cup with a spout, until at last she shook her head, indicating she could drink no more.

"The doctor left some laudanum for you," Susan said, "he said you should have a drop tonight to help you sleep, with the pain in your arm."

Ellen did not care much for laudanum, since she had seen the effects of overindulgence more than once in her work assisting her mother in parish duties. Considering the pain in her arm and her throat, though, she nodded acceptance. Poppy-induced oblivion would be welcome just now.

The bitter taste lingered on her tongue, but she soon found herself drifting off, numbness overwhelming her and washing away the pain. She was on the edge of sleep when Thomas sat down beside the bed again.

"Thomas," she whispered his name, fumbling for his hand. Warm, strong fingers wrapped around hers.

"I'm here. Sleep, Ellen. You're safe, I promise."

She wanted to stay awake, to look on his dear, beloved face, but the poppy had her deep in its thrall. Her eyelids were so heavy. They drifted closed to the sound of Thomas humming a soft, soothing lullaby.

Ellen woke screaming, or trying to, hoarse croaks all that emitted from her bruised throat. Thomas was there at once, strong arms folding around her as he spoke, assuring her she was safe.

Leaning against Thomas' strong chest, Ellen remembered the other reason why she did not care for laudanum. Her mother had given it to her when she was ten or so and had an infected tooth. The nightmares had woken her screaming five times that horrible night. What she had dreamed, she could not say; nameless horrors with sharp teeth and tearing claws teased the edges of her consciousness.

"It's all right," Thomas was whispering, stroking her hair, and she realised he had moved to sit on the edge of the bed, the better to comfort her. Daringly, she put her arm about his waist and leaned in closer, feeling to her amazement the way he placed kisses against her hair and brow.

The room was quite dark, lit only by the faint glow of the banked fire and a single candlestick on her dresser.

"What time is it?" she whispered finally.

"Sometime after midnight. I sent Susan to get some sleep; do you need anything?"

She shook her head against his chest. "It was just a nightmare." Her eyelids were already beginning to droop again.

"Sleep," Thomas told her softly. "You're quite safe, I promise." He kissed her hair again and drew her gently down to lie among the pillows. Comforted by his warmth, Ellen snuggled close to him and let herself drift off again.

"My lord, the doctor is here."

Susan's voice woke Ellen from slumber; she was warm and comfortable, and quite disinclined to move. Unfortunately, her bed seemed to have other ideas, as it shifted beneath her.

"What the… oh." Opening her eyes, she discovered it was not her bed which was moving, but Thomas, upon whose chest she was currently reclining. He shot her a sheepish smile as he laid her back gently against the pillows, and she looked around the room, face flaming. Only Susan appeared to be witness to their very compromising situation, though, and the maid stood with face averted, firmly not looking at them.

"I'll just go and make myself presentable," Thomas told Susan quietly as she passed. "I'll wait outside; please call me in once the doctor has completed his examination."

Ellen was, for the first time, grateful for her sore throat, because it meant she had an excellent excuse not to try and explain away the unexplainable. Susan appeared quite happy to pretend she had seen nothing untoward, in any case, as she bustled about tidying the room and helping Ellen to sit up, re-brushing her hair and pulling it back into a loose braid.

"There you go, Miss." Susan gave her a warm smile, patting her hand lightly. "I'll bring the doctor in now, shall I?"

Ellen didn't remember meeting Doctor Smithee the previous evening, but his quiet manner inspired confidence, and she lay back to allow him to inspect her throat with gentle fingers. He did not unwrap the bandage about her arm, but asked her how it was feeling and listened gravely to her whispered answer.

"Unless you begin to feel heat in it, or start running a fever, I think we shall leave that to itself for a few days yet," he said finally. "The witch hazel compresses are doing their job to minimise the bruising on your throat, which frankly was my most immediate concern. Severe swelling there might restrict your breathing. Keep them up for two more days at least," he instructed Susan, who nodded quick acceptance of the order.

"My voice?" Ellen whispered. She could barely get a sound out; even attempting to shout produced nothing more than a faint croak, and a painful one at that.

"Patience, my dear." Doctor Smithee twinkled at her. "Nasty bruises take a few days to heal, don't they? Well, in a few days I believe you will find your voice beginning to return. Plenty of soothing tea to drink and soup to drink until you feel able to take something firmer. I believe you should be your own best guide, as regards your return to health; I have no doubt Lord Havers will be keeping a close eye to ensure you do not do too much, at any rate."

Ellen smiled shyly and ducked her head at the mention of Thomas' name, and the doctor nodded, stepping back.

"Indeed, I have no doubt his Lordship is waiting outside the door at this very moment, agitating to be let back in so he may quiz me as to the progress of your recovery. Admit him, if you would, my good woman," he addressed Susan, who hurried to the door to do his bidding.

Chapter Fifteen

Once Doctor Smithee departed, Thomas lost no time in settling back down on the bed beside Ellen again, drawing her into his arms. With a shy glance at Susan, who studiously ignored them, Ellen settled her head on his chest. She had questions to ask, but for now, it felt so good just to be held close and safe in Thomas' arms.

Finally, she whispered "What happens now?"

"For us?" Thomas asked, brushing a gentle kiss over her brow.

"Louisa, Clarice, too." Though she had wracked her brain, Ellen could see no way out of the current situation without some sort of scandal enveloping the family, one Thomas did not deserve.

"Ah. Yes. Well, I have sent off an inquiry to the hospital the good doctor told me about on the Isle of Wight, and I hope to hear back from them in a few days. Should they be able to accept Louisa for treatment, I will have to escort her there. Clarice has expressed a desire to remain close to her daughter, so she will accompany us and I will find her a house, set her up with some servants and the like."

Ellen squeezed his hand, glad of his consideration, but questions still remained. What would people say if Louisa and Clarice just up and vanished in the middle of the Little Season?

"As to what story we should put about, I had a thought on that subject I wished to run by you," Thomas said, almost as though he had read her mind. "Obviously, letting it be known that Louisa is dangerously insane is… not ideal."

She snorted at the understatement, though it made her cough.

"So I thought we could tell people she ran away with a footman."

Ellen choked. Wide-eyed, she stared at Thomas, who chuckled at her reaction. He was absolutely serious, she realised as he spoke again.

"Clarice, obviously, will choose to retire from society in shame. She intends to live secluded on the

Isle of Wight anyway, and anyone who might recognise her or Louisa while visiting relatives of their own at the asylum is unlikely to speak out."

Though the idea seemed wild at first, Ellen soon saw the sense in it. She touched her throat, though, and looked at Thomas with questioning eyes.

"Yes, we shall have to remain in seclusion until your throat has healed," Thomas agreed, "though a case of the influenza would explain both the doctor's visits and our absence from Society for a few days at least. Easy enough to have Mr Henry tell anyone who calls that you, Clarice and I are all afflicted, and for Louisa to 'take advantage' of our illnesses to 'run away' with her lover."

It was actually a very clever plan, Ellen thought as she ran through some of the issues in her mind. While it would certainly be a scandal, Louisa would hardly be the first heiress to disgrace herself with a lover from the servant classes, and Clarice retiring from society would be a perfectly natural reaction to her daughter's fall from grace.

"The servants?" she asked hoarsely, glancing across at where Susan was now sitting by the window quietly sewing.

"Have no wish to see the Havers family as a whole disgraced by the madness of one member. You have endeared yourself to them greatly, Ellen; you should have heard the celebrating below stairs when Susan told them our news. I believe I have been congratulated by almost every member of the staff on my excellent choice of bride."

She blushed at the compliment and cast her eyes down shyly. Thomas waited patiently for her to look back at him, at which point he took the opportunity to steal a kiss.

Ellen was even redder when he moved back, and he chuckled warmly. "You have to marry me now, anyway. You are hopelessly compromised, not that anyone who knows would ever breathe a word of it."

She expressed her opinion of his poor humour with a light slap to his arm. Thomas smiled before continuing.

"And we have the perfect ally to help us sell the story. Your new friend Lady Jersey."

Ellen gave him a wide-eyed look of dread. Lady Jersey's reputation as a gossip was unparalleled; if she didn't buy the story, they were doomed. She would undoubtedly dig until she uncovered the truth, and she had the resources and the contacts to root it out.

On the other hand, Lady Jersey had shown no particular liking for Louisa, or Clarice. If Ellen and

Thomas offered her a salacious piece of gossip—delivered with suitable regret, of course, for a situation that could not be helped and a scandal that could not be hidden—why would she look any further?

"You seem to have thought it all through very well," Ellen whispered at last.

"It is merely the bones of a plan, Ellen, and one I would not even think of executing without talking it over with you first. You know well that from the very first, I have valued your counsel above all others. Doing this without your approval is unthinkable."

Ellen reached up to touch his face in gentle wonder. He'd obviously had his valet shave him while the doctor attended her, for his cheek was smooth, her fingertips skating lightly over his skin.

"I love you, Thomas," she whispered.

The expression on Thomas' face was one of pure joy and adoration as he pulled her closer and kissed her again, this time until she thought she might swoon from sheer delight.

"Ahem," Susan said eventually, and Thomas let Ellen go with a quiet laugh.

"Do not fear, Susan, I do not intend to ravish Ellen before we have said our vows in a church."

"I would never doubt you, my lord," Susan replied, a thread of laughter in her voice.

"Excellent, Susan. Excellent. I believe you deserve a promotion for your loyal service, in fact; how does being the Countess of Havers' personal maid sound to you?"

"As long as it is the future countess and not the present one, I shall be delighted and honoured, my lord," Susan said gravely.

Laughing hurt too much, so Ellen swallowed it down and rested her head against Thomas' shoulder again. Her eyelids felt heavy, and she realised sleep was approaching once more.

"Sleep," Thomas whispered, kissing her cheek tenderly. "I will have more news once you wake up again. For now, I need you to rest, regain your strength. I will need your wise counsel when you wake, if we are to pull this off."

The plan to remove Louisa and Clarice to the Isle of Wight went off without a hitch. Thomas had his secretary write polite refusals to all invitations they received, explaining that influenza had laid them all low, and the staff told anyone who asked the same.

Doctor Smithee's regular visits to the house only confirmed the fact in everyone's minds.

Clarice came to see Ellen once before their departure. "I'm sorry," was all she managed to say, through tears streaming down her cheeks. "I hope you and Thomas will be happy together, truly." She could not look at Ellen directly as she spoke.

"I hope Louisa finds peace," was all Ellen could think of to say. She pitied Clarice deeply, but the older woman's decisions made to protect her daughter had almost caused Ellen's demise, and even with Ellen's forgiving nature she could not find it in herself to entirely absolve Clarice of guilt.

Thomas had to escort Clarice and Louisa to their destination, of course. They slipped out of London in a closed carriage, one without the family crest emblazoned on it, late one night. Still weak and easily exhausted, Thomas made Ellen promise to remain in bed until he returned, charging the servants with her welfare. He hated leaving her, but there was nothing for it; she was not well enough to travel and he had to see Clarice and Louisa settled. Sending Mr Gallagher ahead to arrange Louisa's residency at the psychiatric hospital and have a house arranged for Clarice would, Thomas hoped, minimise the amount of time he would need to spend on the island.

Doctor Smithee had prescribed herbs and teas which they had been using to keep Louisa calm ever since her attack on Ellen, and she spent the journey in a quiet, dreamlike haze. Once or twice she murmured something about 'a honeymoon by the seaside' and Thomas realised she thought they were married, or soon to be so. Not wishing to disrupt her calm state of mind, he said nothing to contradict her, but made sure to keep his distance, riding alongside the carriage rather than in it for most of the journey.

The hospital was in a large, elegantly appointed country house close to the centre of the island. Considering the fees they charged to enrol patients, the property should be well maintained, Thomas considered, and was pleased to note the exceptional cleanliness of every room. While the residents were permitted to mingle with each other, they did so only under supervision, and no resident was allowed to roam alone outside or to leave the estate's grounds under any circumstances.

"You should go," Clarice told Thomas quietly as Louisa inspected the large, well-appointed suite set aside for her personal use. Her 'maid' was a specially trained nurse, a large, no-nonsense countrywoman with a thick Hampshire accent who was well aware of Louisa's occasional violent proclivities, and, she assured Thomas privately, well-equipped to handle them.

"You have not seen your house yet," Thomas protested.

"I'll not leave Louisa here alone yet. Her rage when you leave will be ugly enough to witness; I may be able to calm her somewhat. Once she is settled here, I'll have the carriage take me to the house. You have been more than kind, Thomas, giving me my own carriage and arranging all this."

Clarice seemed a different woman, Thomas thought. Yet, what would she have done to conceal Louisa's terrible secret, if she had been able? Her silence almost cost Ellen's life, and he could not, would not trust her. He had already assigned a man to ensure neither she nor Louisa would ever find passage back to the mainland without his express authority.

With a last look at Louisa, examining a delicate writing-desk fully fitted out for her with papers, pens and ink—though any letters she sent would never reach their destination, unless it was to him—Thomas nodded.

"Take care, Clarice. If there is anything you ever need—anything at all—I pray you will let me know at once."

She did not offer an embrace, only inclined her head regally and said a single word.

"Goodbye."

Chapter Sixteen

Thomas did not hide his return to London. Supposedly, he was arriving back after a frantic attempt to intercept Louisa before reaching Scotland with her lowborn lover, after all. Late that day, a closed carriage would depart the house, and he would tell anyone who asked that Clarice was in it, leaving to be with her daughter as they settled in an undisclosed location.

For now, all he could think of was Ellen, as he handed the reins of his tired horse to a groom who wished him a good day. Taking the steps to the house two at a time, he strode past the smiling Mr Henry and headed for the interior stairs.

"Not that way, my lord!" Mr Henry called after him.

"I beg your pardon?" Thomas paused, one foot on the bottom step.

"In the parlour, my lord." Mr Henry gestured. "I daresay you don't need me to present you?"

The butler was talking to thin air.

Ellen looked up from her book as the parlour door opened. A second later the book fell unheeded to the floor as she leaped to her feet, and a second after that she was rushing into Thomas' arms, heedless of any audience who might observe them.

"Ellen," he kept saying as he rained kisses on her face, "my Ellen, how I've missed you!"

Ellen could find no words, too choked with emotion to speak. She clung tightly to Thomas and closed her eyes, revelling in the solid strength of him as he held her close.

"You should not be out of bed," Thomas said finally, pulling back to hold her at arm's length, his palms cupped over her shoulders.

Ellen laughed. The sound was husky yet, but she could speak and make herself heard. Although the bruises on her throat were still livid with colour, they were green and yellow rather than black and purple, clearly ageing and fading away. "I have been pampered and waited on hand and foot ever since you left, Thomas. Today is the first day Susan has even permitted me to leave my room, and that only because I protested I would run mad if I did not see something other than those four walls."

Hearing her speak, sounding almost like her old self, Thomas smiled in relief. He still led her back to the comfortable fireside chair she had been occupying, though, settling her down in it and seating himself on the footstool, keeping her hands held in his.

"Obviously you are on the mend. Has Doctor Smithee been attentive?"

"Here every day at least once, sometimes twice." Ellen smiled at him, pulling one of her hands free and reaching to touch his cheek. "How are you, Thomas?"

"I'm not the one who was injured."

"No, but you have still had a long journey, and I have no doubt settling Louisa and Clarice did not go entirely smoothly. So I ask again; how are you?"

He stared into her eyes for a long moment before bowing his head and laying it in her lap. "Did I do the right thing, Ellen?"

"It was the only thing you could do," she replied at once, stroking her fingers through his hair tenderly. "I have thought on it a great deal, since you left; I have had little else to do other than think, and no matter how many different possibilities I considered, none of them ended any better than the path you chose."

Thomas sighed deeply, nodding slowly against her lap. "I know. I have had a good deal of time to think too, and I could not think of anything else either. Short of shipping Louisa off somewhere even more remote and locking her in a cottage in the Highlands or something where there is no chance of her ever being seen again by someone who might possibly recognise her…"

"Which would be too cruel a fate, even for her," Ellen said quietly as he trailed off.

"Even if it were not, I believe Clarice would have insisted on going with her, and that would most definitely have been unfair." Thomas lifted his head to look at her. "I know she was unkind to you, Ellen, but she is, after all, family."

"And neither you nor I have so many family members that we are willing to let any of them suffer unnecessarily."

"Exactly." Taking her hand, he pressed a kiss to her fingers. "To tell the truth, my joy in loving you is so all-encompassing, I cannot consider anything which might make anyone in the least distressed."

For a long moment they sat lost in each other's eyes, so glad to be reunited all worldly cares fell away. At last, though, Thomas shook himself and addressed the most pressing item on his mind.

"I tasked Gallagher with obtaining a special licence when I sent him back to town, and if he is half as efficient as I think him to be, it will even now be lying on my desk. Forgive me if it is your dream to have a magnificent wedding at Haverford attended by half the county, but I think it best for us to marry as quickly and quietly as possible, and then to depart London immediately."

"I have no such yearnings, and I quite agree that is the best plan," Ellen said at once. "So long as you are the bridegroom, I find I care not for any other details as to when and where."

Thomas looked delighted by her sentiment, and kissed her hands again. "Have you a gown with a high collar which would conceal your bruises? If so, we might be able to invite a few close friends to witness the nuptials."

Ellen considered that. While she had not been in London long enough to make many friends, she thought she would like to invite Lady Creighton, who had been so kind to her, and the three older ladies who wished to take her under their wing. She felt quite sure they would all be pleased for her to marry Thomas, who they had seemed to look upon with some favour despite his American birth.

Thomas left her briefly to go to his study, where he found both his steward and the special licence the faithful man had efficiently procured. Gallagher was more than happy to go out at once and find an amenable parson to perform the ceremony as soon as possible.

"I have been thinking," Ellen told Thomas as the pair of them ate dinner together that evening, sitting in Ellen's sitting-room with Susan sewing quietly in the corner, "that I should pay a call on Lady Jersey."

Thomas stopped with his soup spoon suspended in mid-air, eyed her uncertainly. "Would it not be better to write to her once we have left London?"

"Except that I should like to invite her to attend the wedding." The ceremony was set for three days' hence, in a small church close by.

Thomas set the spoon down with a sigh. "Well. It was always part of the plan to tell her the public version of events to spread, was it not? I daresay if we do so in person, we will be that much more believable."

Ellen nodded in agreement. "I should like to call on Lady Creighton, too," she said. "She was very kind to me, and indeed, without her interference we might not even be sitting here now. It was her insistence that I not be a wallflower which led me to dance with Lord Bellmere and Major Trevithick, after all."

Thomas narrowed his eyes at her. "Which caused me to realise my own idiocy in not noticing your utter perfection from the very first moment. Indeed, your reproach is valid."

She laughed at him in return. "Do not dare to be jealous, Thomas. Neither of them had any chance of winning my heart, I promise you. It has long been yours."

They gazed at each other until Susan coughed from the corner. "That soup will taste far better while it's hot, m'lord, Miss Bentley," she said in gentle reproach.

"You see, I am well cared for," Ellen smiled at her maid and picked up her spoon again. "Susan has coddled me like a hen with one chick in your absence."

"Good," Thomas said emphatically.

Choosing to change the subject, and given a new one because of Susan's gentle reminder, Ellen remarked on the gossip already beginning to circulate. "The servants have begun spreading the requested story, whispering of Louisa's departure and disgrace with a fictional member of their number." Shaking her head, Ellen said "It's a sad indictment of her behaviour towards them, that they are positively eager to begin crowing of her downfall."

"Let them enjoy their revenge, Ellen. Who knows how many servants Louisa had dismissed, or even hurt more seriously, like that maid Clarice told me about? Frankly, I think we should just be thankful they are not trumpeting the truth of her madness all over London."

"They would not," Ellen denied firmly.

"I happen to agree, mainly because you have endeared yourself so greatly to them, both here and at Havers Hall!"

They paid a call on Lady Jersey the following morning, Ellen's throat well covered by a lacy shawl wrapped high, the huskiness of her voice explained away by the lingering effects of influenza.

The countess asked a few probing questions about Louisa, and Thomas and Ellen answered carefully, their story well-rehearsed. They both expressed regret at their cousin's disgrace, shock at her abrupt departure.

"I had not the slightest idea she planned anything of the sort, I assure you," Ellen told the countess. "I do know Lady Havers was pressing Louisa to settle on one of her suitors; perhaps that prompted her to take her chance when we were all ill abed with influenza."

"Foolish chit." Lady Jersey shook her head. "Well, it is certainly a scandal, but I do not believe it shall touch you particularly. Especially since you plan to marry so soon. You sly thing, Miss Bentley, you gave no hint of that at all!" She tapped Ellen's hand with her fan, chuckling to herself.

Ellen blushed, glanced sideways at Thomas, who grinned at her in return. "In my defence, my lady, I had no idea Thomas returned my affections until after Louisa's disgrace came to light. Emotions were running high at that time."

"No doubt, no doubt." Lady Jersey seemed highly amused. "Well, it is a charming outcome for the pair of you, to be certain, though I quite understand why you feel it necessary to marry quickly and return to the country." Waving a languid hand, she declared "I shall make sure the new Countess of Havers can move in society without any hint of scandal attaching to her from her cousin's foolishness. You leave *that* to *me*."

"We defer to your expertise, of course, Lady Jersey," Thomas said, amused.

"I knew you were a smart young man, Havers, despite hailing from the colonies. You'll do well enough, I dare say."

Ellen stifled a little giggle as Lady Jersey accepted the compliment imperiously. She could only count herself lucky that the formidable lady was disposed to believe their story.

"You will come to the wedding, won't you, Lady Jersey?" she asked hopefully.

"I would not miss it, dear girl, and I shall bring Eliza Sale and Charlotte Peabody with me, and anyone else I can scoop up."

"Oh, thank you," Ellen said gratefully. "We will not have time to call upon everyone who I should have wished to invite, though we go from here to the Creighton townhouse. I should very much like to invite Lady Creighton to attend."

Chapter Seventeen

The day of the wedding dawned dull and raining, though Susan claimed it would clear up later. Refusing to let the weather sour her mood, Ellen smiled and insisted it would not matter if it rained all day. She had no doubt Mr Henry would have arranged things so that no guest would risk so much as a single raindrop touching their hair or clothing.

"Perhaps, but your shoes would be all over mud, miss!" Susan muttered direly. "Come, into your bath and let's get your hair washed and drying in front of the fire. Betty will be bringing your breakfast up directly."

Smiling as her maid took charge, Ellen slipped into the prepared bath and relaxed in the warm water as Susan massaged flakes of Castile soap into her hair before washing it out with apple cider vinegar and a rosemary and lavender rinse.

"I wonder if Thomas is being fussed over as much as I?" she murmured as Susan helped her dry off and slip on a robe.

"I've no doubt he is having a bath, miss. There were a great many jugs of water being warmed by fireplaces all over the house this morning." Susan squeezed water from Ellen's hair with a linen cloth before taking a comb and carefully beginning to separate the strands, using a little lavender oil on her fingers to smooth out tangles. "Though for sure his hair will be quicker for Kenneth to dry!"

For some reason, Ellen found that ridiculously funny. Giggling, she picked up the cup of chocolate Betty had brought with her breakfast tray to take a sip.

"'Tis good to hear you laughing on your wedding day, miss," Susan said. "And look—the rain has stopped!"

"So it has," Ellen agreed, peering out of the window.

"Happy is the bride the sun shines upon," Susan quoted the old saying.

"Perhaps, but my parents were the happiest couple I know and Mama always said it snowed on their wedding day. And it certainly poured with rain the day Demelza and John married, and they are very happy too, so I will not put stock in miserable wedding days having anything to do with unhappy marriages," Ellen declared firmly.

"Very wise too, I dare say," Susan agreed. "Won't you eat something, miss?"

Ellen smiled wryly. Of course her sharp-eyed maid had noticed Ellen had not chosen anything from the tempting array on the tray. "My stomach is in knots, with nerves," she confessed.

"Just think of it like every other wedding your father, God rest his soul, officiated over the years," Susan suggested. "I dare say you've seen more weddings than anyone else in this house!"

That was quite true, Ellen mused as she allowed Susan to coax her into eating a slice of toast spread with butter and honey. Her father always said he loved nothing better than conducting a wedding, seeing a loving couple joined together in matrimony in God's house... unless it was the baptisms which often followed, sometimes a little less than nine months later, though her father would never comment no matter how short the time between wedding and birth.

Her parents would have liked Thomas, she thought, very much. She could imagine he and her father having long debates over what they read in the newspapers, her mother recruiting Thomas into helping with one of her projects to improve the lot of the poorest villagers.

A tear trickled from her eye, and she blotted it away. "I am just thinking of Mama and Papa," she replied to Susan's concerned query. "I wish they were here."

"Of course you do, miss. No doubt they'll be watching over you from heaven, though," Susan said stoutly, and Ellen nodded.

"No doubt," she agreed quietly. No doubt the old Earl would be rolling over in his grave, too, if he could see his upstart American heir marrying the impoverished parson's daughter he had never deigned to acknowledge as his relation, but she did not voice that thought aloud.

The servants had filled the little church with foliage, purchasing all the hothouse blooms they could find with Thomas' purse opened for the purpose, and adding beautifully woven wreaths of greenery. The sweet scent of the blossoms filled

Ellen's nose as she took a deep breath before stepping over the threshold of the church.

Smiling faces greeted her, the servants at the back of the church and a surprising number of higher society at the front as she walked up the aisle. Lady Jersey, in a position of honour in the front row, was positively beaming, Lady Sale and Mrs Peabody beside her looking just as pleased to see Ellen married. Marianne Creighton was directly behind them, her older husband at her side looking less than pleased with the occasion, but Marianne's smile was bright. Ellen thought she would be sure to write Marianne very often. Lady Creighton seemed very much in need of a friend.

At last, she reached the end of the seemingly interminable walk to where Thomas awaited her before the altar, a broad grin on his face. Seeing how joyous he looked soothed the butterflies in Ellen's stomach and she smiled happily back at him, the last of her worries falling away.

Together, she thought as she placed her hand in Thomas's and the curate began intoning the words to the marriage ceremony, they would deal with whatever trials and tribulations might come their way. They might well set the Ton on its ear with their new-fangled ideas and determination that the common folk should be treated just the same as the aristocracy, but Ellen found she did not care in the slightest what the spoiled scions of the upper class might think of them, and she knew Thomas did not either.

"I love you," Thomas mouthed as the curate droned on.

"I love you too," Ellen mouthed back.

"If any man here knows any reason why this couple should not be joined together in holy matrimony," the curate said, frowning at them both, "let him speak now, or forever hold his peace."

For a wild moment, Ellen half-expected Louisa to leap from behind one of the pews, knife in hand, and she flinched slightly. Thomas tightened his grasp on her hand, concern entering his expression, but she shook her head and smiled at him again.

The church was absolutely quiet. Thomas smiled reassuringly back at Ellen, perhaps guessing something of what she was thinking, and the curate began the ceremony again, this time preparing them to speak their vows.

"I now pronounce you to be man and wife in the sight of God," the curate ended at last. "My lords, ladies and gentlemen, the Earl and Countess of Havers."

"My lady," Thomas said with a smile, and Ellen laughed delightedly.

"Your lady indeed, my lord!"

Uncaring in the least whether they scandalised their audience, Thomas drew her close to place a lingering kiss on her lips. A few tuts sounded from the most traditional, but almost all the congregation beamed at the happy couple, glad to see Ellen find happiness with her Earl at last.

A Note From The Author

An Earl For Ellen is the first in the *Blushing Brides* series. Look out for *A Marquis For Marianne*, Book 2 in the series, also available now!

I hope you enjoyed reading *An Earl For Ellen*. If you did, I hope you will consider leaving a review of the book on Amazon or Goodreads, so that other potential readers can see your recommendation!

With thanks and best wishes

Catherine Bilson

Brisbane, Australia
January 2019